PLAYING WITH FIRE

Also by Kiki Swinson

The Playing Dirty Series: *Playing Dirty* and *Notorious*
The Candy Shop
A Sticky Situation
The Wifey Series: *Wifey, I'm Still Wifey, Life After Wifey,*
Still Wifey Material
Wife Extraordinaire Series: *Wife Extraordinaire* and *Wife*
Extraordinaire Returns
Cheaper to Keep Her Series: Books 1–5
The Score Series: *The Score* and *The Mark*
Dead on Arrival
The Black Market Series: *The Black Market, The Safe*
House, Property of the State
The Deadline
Public Enemy #1
Playing with Fire

ANTHOLOGIES
Sleeping with the Enemy (with Wahida Clark)
Heist and *Heist 2* (with De'nesha Diamond)
Lifestyles of the Rich and Shameless (with Noire)
A Gangster and a Gentleman (with De'nesha Diamond)
Most Wanted (with Nikki Turner)
Still Candy Shopping (with Amaleka McCall)
Fistful of Benjamins (with De'nesha Diamond)
Schemes and *Dirty Tricks* (with Saundra)
Bad Behavior (with Noire)

Published by Kensington Publishing Corp.

PLAYING WITH FIRE

KIKI SWINSON

urban fiction

DAFINA

www.kensingtonbooks.com

DAFINA BOOKS are published by

Kensington Publishing Corp.
119 West 40th Street
New York, NY 10018

All Kensington Titles, Imprints, and Distributed Lines are available at special quantity discounts for bulk purchases for sales promotions, premiums, fund-raising, and educational or institutional use. Special book excerpts or customized printings can also be created to fit specific needs. For details, write or phone the office of the Kensington special sales manager: Kensington Publishing Corp., 119 West 40th Street, New York, NY 10018, attn: Special Sales Department, Phone: 1-800-221-2647.

Library of Congress Card Catalogue Number: 2021940069

The DAFINA logo is a trademark of Kensington Publishing Corp.

ISBN: 978-1-4967-3411-2
First Kensington Hardcover Edition: December 2021

ISBN: 978-1-4967-3417-4 (ebook)

10 9 8 7 6 5 4 3 2 1

Printed in the United States of America

PLAYING WITH FIRE

The Beginning

I knew at first glance that my roommate Gia Santos had snorted a couple of lines of coke right before I'd opened the door to our dorm room and walked in. Luckily for her, I didn't show up with one of the other girls who lived in the building. Occasionally, one or two of my dorm neighbors would follow me back to my room to borrow a textbook, and today would not have been a good day. She looked out of it. Dazed. She blinked a few times to readjust her eyes.

"What's eating you?" she asked me as she opened her eyes wide.

I slammed the door of our room and took a seat on the edge of my bed. "I swear, Professor Reynolds is going to make me put a hit out on him if he keeps fucking with me," I spat.

"What happened?" She asked the question, but judging from her facial expression, she could not have cared less about my problem with our professor. She tilted her head back and closed her eyes.

"Come on now, Gia, really?!" I whined.

She lifted her head and looked at me. "What?" she said.

"You're not even listening to me."

"Yes, I am," she added as she focused her eyes on me. She tried her best to pretend that she was being attentive.

"What grade did he give you for your exam?"

"He gave me a 92," she replied, stretching her neck to the side.

"Wait, how did you get a better grade than me? We studied together."

"I let him eat me out right before class this morning."

"Oh, so you're back at that again, huh?" I commented. I was repulsed by the idea that she would even let him come near her in that way.

"You better get with the program, or you're gonna get left behind," she warned me. And within seconds she closed her eyes again and lay back on her bed. This time she was out like a light.

I couldn't sit there and watch her go off into a zone while I wallowed in my state of depression. My mother was going to kill me if she found out that I was failing my classes miserably. She may even be a bitch and pull me out of school altogether. Teach me a lesson, and God knows that I don't want her to do that. My dad passed away a few years ago in a bad car accident, so the only parent breathing down my throat is my mother. What will I do? Go back home and sit around and watch her berate my stepfather? Boss our housekeeper around unnecessarily?

I swear, my mom could be the meanest person alive sometimes. It's like she prides herself on being a bitch. No one likes her. Even I don't like her. I deal with her crazy ass only because she's my mom and it's written somewhere in the Bible that you're supposed to honor your mother and father.

College spring break would be here in two days, and I wasn't looking forward to flying back to New York to see her. My dad's side of the family lives here in Norfolk, Virginia, but I'm not close to them, so what other choices did I have?

Instead of moping around in my dorm room, I grabbed my purse and left. I figured I needed to get something to take my mind off all the bad shit I had going on in my life.

On my way out of my building, I walked into Rita Reznik. She wasn't alone. Three frat boys wearing their fraternity jackets were walking by as well. It was Conner, Eric, and Tyler. They were the popular white boys from ODU's Division I football team, so they were the cream of the crop. The most admired by other guys and desired by most girls. Each one was cute. But they were dogs, and yet girls always threw themselves at them.

"What's up, Yoshi? When are you gonna let me spend some time with you?" Conner flirted.

"Yeah, you should come and hang out with us," Tyler said.

"Wait, Conner, aren't you screwing the brains out of her roommate Gia?" Rita teased them.

"Who is that?" he said jokingly. "And besides, what's wrong with the two-for-one special?" He continued to clown around.

"She'll be interested in me once I show her what I'm working with," Tyler added as he grabbed and tugged on his genitals.

Eric chuckled in the background and started blowing kisses at me.

"Sorry, but I don't fuck little boys with little dicks!" I shot back at them.

"I'm sorry but you got me mixed up with somebody else. I've got the biggest dick you'll ever find on a white boy," he boasted.

"I find that hard to believe," Rita joked as they continued walking by.

"Hey guys, sounds like Rita is trying to keep Yoshi to herself, huh?" Conner called out.

"It seems that way to me too," Eric chimed in.

"Rita, *cock blocker* would look really nice on your resume," Conner commented.

"Right under 'the campus Xanax and Ecstasy dealer who makes the bulk of her money from a group of dumb-ass frat boys.'"

"Piss off!" Rita replied, and stuck up her middle finger.

"Yeah, yeah, yeah . . ." Tyler added as they moved on in the other direction.

"They're such jerk-offs," Rita commented as she approached me. She's hot shit on campus. She was pretty too. If you stood her next to Janet Jackson, you couldn't tell them apart. Word around campus is that her brother was a prescription drug dealer and her father was a coke dealer. I wouldn't be shocked about it. I mean, where else would she get the drugs she sells around campus? There's no prescription drug that she doesn't have. Gia is one of her customers. I cop from her too. But not as much as Gia and a couple of other girls in my dorm. I mentioned to Gia a time or two that she needed to be careful around campus. We had a lot of haters roaming around who would love to see her arrested and put out of school.

"What's up with you? Why the long face?" she asked me.

"Professor Reynolds gave me a shitty grade on my exam, and my mom is going to shit in her pants when she finds out."

"What did you get?"

"A freaking 72."

"Don't sweat it. I'm gonna take care of that for you," she said confidently.

"And how are you going to do that?"

"I told you not to worry. I got it."

I let out a long sigh. "You sure?"

"Yes, now let me get out of here. I've gotta get to my next class."

"Thank you so much! I owe you."

"I'm gonna hold you to that." She chuckled and walked away.

Hearing Rita say that she would take care of my situation took a load off my back. All I could do was wait.

It wouldn't shock me if I found out that my mother had someone watching me, because as soon as I walked away from Rita and stepped foot back in my dorm room, our room phone rang. When I answered it I found out it was my mother.

"Hi, Mom."

"Hi," she replied quickly, and then she went into question mode. "What time does your flight arrive? I don't want your stepfather to waste time waiting on you when he could be doing something else." My mom never minced her words. She was a straight shooter and didn't care who liked it.

"The time on my ticket says that I'll get there at five thirty-five p.m.," I replied.

"Are you staying here for your entire spring break?"

"That's the plan." It took everything within me to answer that question. She has this way of talking to me like she doesn't want to be bothered.

"Do you have any special requests or things I could get for you before you get here?"

"No, you know I'm a simple person. The regular fried chicken and eggs and turkey bacon is all I need."

"You know I don't eat greasy food. It's bad for you," she pointed out.

"Has Sydney stopped eating chicken?"

"No, he hasn't. But I have gotten him to eat baked chicken. There's a couple of soul food places around here that sells it."

"Where is he now?" I asked her. I'd learned over the years that if you continue to harp on a subject too long with my mother, she will dominate the conversation.

"Visiting his parents down in Florida."

"How are they doing?"

"You're gonna have to ask him. I don't meddle in the affairs dealing with his parents. They have a weird dynamic. All I ever hear them say to each other is how much they love each other. His mother calls at least ten times a day. She carries on like he's a teenager. It's annoying."

I chuckled.

"What's so funny?" She said it in a way like, how dare I laugh. What she said had no humor in it.

"Oh, it's nothing really." I downplayed it. "So when is he coming home?"

"He'll be back tomorrow."

"Wow! So you've got to make two trips to the airport?"

"Oh no, honey. He drove himself to the airport. You know I don't do a lot of unnecessary driving."

"Your anniversary is right around the corner. "

"Yes, it is."

"Have you two decided where you're going this year?"

"Spain," she replied with no enthusiasm.

I know if someone told me that they were taking me out of the country, I would be ecstatic. "How long are you guys going to be there?"

"Seven days and six nights."

"That sounds fun. Wish I had someone to take me to Spain." I said jokingly. I wanted my mother to be happy knowing that her husband was taking her out of the country. He was very wealthy and spared no expense in going all out for my mother. I just had to convince her that she needs to be a little more grateful.

"How's school?" She abruptly changed the subject.

"School is going great," I forced myself to say cheerfully.

But my mother was no fool. She raised me, so she knows when I am lying to her. "How did you do on your last exam?" She pressed the issue.

"Not sure. Haven't gotten my score yet."

"Think you'll get it before you leave for break?"

"I should."

"How do you think you did?" She wouldn't let up.

"I feel like I did great," I replied enthusiastically. Once again, I had to act as if everything on my end was on course even though it wasn't.

"I hope so. Sydney and I are spending a lot of money sending you to that university, so don't let us down."

I let out a long sigh. "I know, Mom."

"Don't get smart with me."

"I'm not. But you keep saying the same thing over and over," I pointed out. What I really wanted to say was that Sydney was the only one forking over the money to send me to school. But I left well enough alone. I knew she'd leave me stranded at the airport if I told her what I really wanted to say.

"And I will say it over and over again if I feel like you need to hear it," she spat. "Now let me get off this phone before I say something else."

"Okay, see you in a couple of days," I managed to say before she ended our call.

I headed to my friend Maria's dorm room so we could chat. She was a political science major like me. We had a few classes together. Her career goal was to become an FBI agent. I couldn't see it because she was so laid-back. She was a beautiful and down-to-earth twenty-year-old. Now don't get it twisted, because she was feisty and she made sure that everybody knew it.

"What's up?" she asked after I'd knocked and she'd opened her door.

"I need to blow off some steam," I replied as I walked by her and entered her room.

"What happened?" she wondered out loud and closed the door to her room.

"Professor Reynolds gave me a shitty grade on my exam today," I hissed as I sat down on a chair placed by the desk. I was livid.

"What did he give you?" Maria took a seat on the edge of her bed.

"A 72."

"He can be a fucking dickhead at times."

"Tell me about it."

"Aren't you leaving for spring break the day after tomorrow?"

"Yeah," I reluctantly said.

"You don't sound like you're up for it."

"Am I ever?"

"How is she?"

"Miserable," I began. "She just never seems happy. She wakes up every day and acts like she hates the world, and I'm over it."

"Look at it like this, at least you don't have to be there with her every morning when she wakes up."

"I can always count on you to see the good in everything," I told her, because it was true. Maria stayed away from negativity.

She smiled.

"So when do you leave for Florida?" I changed the subject. Maria's family were immigrants from the Dominican Republic. Maria was born here in America. She was the first generation from her family to go to college. Her family was proud, especially since she was given an academic scholarship.

"I'm leaving right after my last class tomorrow," she told me.

"I know they're gonna be happy to see you."

"They always are when I go to see them."

"I wish I could get that same treatment."

"How many times have I told you to get her to go to counseling?"

Before I could answer Maria's question, one of her roommates walked in the room. Her name was Abby Blum. She was a Jewish girl from a very wealthy family. She was from New York but had a few relatives here in Virginia. Her family owned a lot of real estate around town. You'd think she'd flaunt their wealth, but she didn't. Nothing about her was over the top or flashy. In fact, she walked around with what seemed like the same gray hoodie and sweatpants every day. Maria boasted all the time about how smart this girl was. I'd thought about asking Abby to help me out on term papers a few times, but I can't deal with rejection so I did them on my own.

"Hi," she greeted me as she dropped her backpack on her bed and sat down beside it. She sounded winded. "You guys going to the dining hall?"

"Not me. I've gotta finish packing my stuff," Maria answered first.

"I'm not leaving campus until the day after tomorrow, but I'm sick of eating pizza and Chinese food," I replied.

"Well, I'm not." She chuckled. "I'm gonna get me a personal pan pizza and savor every bit of it." She grabbed her wallet and then left the room.

"She's sweet," I commented.

"Yeah, and she's hardly ever in this room."

"I wish that I could say the same for my roommate. Every time I turn around, she's lying around like there's nothing to do outside our room."

"She's probably high," Maria interjected.

I didn't respond. I looked down at my right foot and started wiggling it like I got a sudden itch.

"Don't act like you didn't hear me," she pressed.

I looked up from my foot. "What are you talking about?"

Maria gave me a hard stare. "Wait, is she still popping pills?" She wouldn't let up. She disliked Gia from the day she met her. And she had good reason too.

"The last time I checked, no."

"Yoshi, don't lie to me."

"I'm not lying. She told me that after her parents found out about her addiction, they put her in outpatient substance abuse classes," I managed to say. Now I can't say how I was able to come up with that terrific story, but it worked, because it got Maria off my damn back. Not only that, Maria doesn't know that I get high with Gia sometimes. If she knew, I was sure she'd stop being my friend and probably rat us out to the dean. Things would end chaotropic if that cat was let out of the bag, and I couldn't let that happen.

Maria and I talked a little while longer, and then I left so she could get ready for her trip back home.

On my way back to my room, I saw flyers posted on every wall asking for help to find a missing girl named Kristen Chambers. According to the flyer, she was a student at the university who had been missing for a month now. I didn't know the girl, but seeing that she was missing and that there was a possibility that she could be dead was terrifying. She was a pretty biracial girl who looked like me. We were almost the same height and weight. The flyer said that she was last seen when she left campus to go to a 7-Eleven store.

Reading this melted my heart away. I knew her family must be going through it. "That's sad, huh?" said a voice from out of nowhere.

I turned around and saw a black girl standing behind me. I swear, I had no idea where she came from. "Yes, it is," I replied. "Do you know her?" I stepped back so I could stand next to her.

"No, I didn't know her. But whoever did this to her, I hope they pay for it dearly." While she expressed her feelings about the situation, I looked at her from head to toe. She was a very petite average-looking girl who couldn't have been older than nineteen. She wore a simple ponytail, sweatshirt, and a pair of blue denim jeans. She looked just like a college kid.

"What's your name?" I asked her.

"Penny. Penny Nelson," she replied, and then she held out her hand.

"Hi, Penny, my name is Yoshi. Yoshi Lomax." I shook her hand. "Which dorm did she live in?"

"The one next to this one."

"Wow! I know her family must be going through it. I know my parents would be going insane if this was me," I said, even though that was false. It sounded good though. "Do you know who her roommates are?" I added.

"I see them around on campus, but that's about it."

"This is strange because I can't believe that I'm just now hearing about this."

"Local and FBI agents have all swarmed this campus asking students and professors if they had any information on her whereabouts."

"Damn! Where was I?" I commented.

"They talked to me," she confessed.

"What did they say?"

"They wanted to know if I knew her. And if I had seen her on the day she was reported missing."

"Did they walk around to every dorm?"

"As far as I know they did."

"Do you live in this building?" I wanted to know.

"Yes, I live on the top floor."

"How long have you been living there?"

"A year now. But I took a semester off to figure out my life, and now I'm back."

"Really?"

She nodded.

"I wonder why I've never seen you before," I questioned out loud. It was becoming clear that I was clueless about everything going on around me, and that's not good.

"It might be because you're very pretty and popular and everybody is always looking at you," she responded.

Taken aback by her comment, I had to replay what she had just said. I mean, I know that I'm very attractive, but what made her think that I'm popular? I didn't hang out with a clique of girls.

"Why do you think I'm popular?" I needed some clarity, because it was clear that she knew something I didn't.

"You don't hear what the girls around campus are saying about you? Every time you enter a room, girls are always talking about how pretty you are. They even wonder what ethnicity you are."

"I'm Asian and black."

"I even hear the guys talk about how much they want you."

"No way," I said, because this girl was blowing my mind. I wasn't getting all the attention that she claimed. Okay, now I was cool with a few groups on campus but not to the extent that she was saying. And to hear her claim that she's around every time people talk about me spooked the hell out of me, so it was time to make my exit.

"Yes, way," she replied in a weird way, and then she just stood there.

I swear, I am a very outspoken girl and for the first time in my life I didn't know what to say to this person in front of me. She had this Norman Bates horror film thing going on. It was really uncomfortable. "Let me get out of here. Gotta pack my things for spring break," I managed to say, and then I grabbed the flyer of the girl off the wall so I could take it with me.

"Talk to you later," she said, still standing there.

"Talk to you later," I replied, and was off in the wind.

I was so happy and relieved that I had finally got away from that weird-ass girl. It wouldn't have surprised me if she was on meds. I mean, who walks around and watches everyone's moves? Who has time to do that? That girl was definitely a nutcase.

I was so glad that Gia was up when I got back. She was on her laptop when I entered into the room. I walked over to her bed and handed her the flyer of the missing girl. "Did you know about this?" I asked after she took the flyer and looked at it.

"Yeah, I heard about it. Why? Have they found her yet?"

"No. I don't think so."

"So why you give the flyer to me?"

"Because this was my first time seeing it."

Gia tossed the flyer next to her on the bed and then continued doing what she was doing on her laptop. "I told the cops that I saw her a couple of times but I didn't know her personally."

I sat down on the edge of my bed and let out a long sigh.

"Think she might be dead?" I wondered aloud.

"She probably is. They said that she was from Connecticut."

"Why you have to say it like that?" I questioned her.

"Say it like what?" Gia seemed puzzled.

"When I asked you if you thought she was dead, you said that she probably was," I pointed out.

"And what was wrong with that?" she replied nonchalantly.

"You said it like you didn't care."

"That's because I don't. I've got too much shit going on in my life to be worried about a girl that I don't know, Yoshi. Why do you think I get high?" She paused and then said, "Because I've got a lot of shit going on in my life that I don't want to deal with. So if you're looking for me to go with you to that girl's pity party, then count me out, because my plate is full."

"I didn't come in here to fight with you. And I didn't ask you to go to a pity party either. I just wanted you to be a little bit more sympathetic about that girl's disappearance. That's all. I know you mean well, so I'm sorry."

"I'm sorry too," she admitted.

After Gia and I closed the chapter about the missing girl, I took off my sneakers and lay back on my bed. I tried to think about the good times that I used to have with my mother back when I was a child, but I couldn't come up with any. I even tried to rehearse in my mind how I was going to take the high road when she started talking out the side of her neck about something I did wrong or how I should live my life. But I came up empty. Listening to Gia tap the keys on her laptop was kind of distracting too. "Hey, Gia, do you know a girl named Penny?" I sparked up a conversation.

"Penny who?" she asked and halted her typing.

"Penny Nelson. She said that she lived on the top floor. Black girl. Skinny. She wears her hair in a ponytail. She said she's been in the building for two years," I said, hoping to jog Gia's memory.

"I think I know who you're talking about. What about her?"

"I was looking at the flyer about the missing girl and she comes up behind me and gives me the whole rundown. She tells me that the cops and the FBI spoke to her about the girl and then somehow she starts telling me how popular I am and that all the girls on campus want to be me—"

"What?" Gia interjected. She seemed confused.

"That's what I said, and then she said how the guys wanted me. I mean, she kept going on and on. I had to get away from her because she was freaking me out."

"She sounds weird."

"I thought the same thing."

"Who are you guys talking about?" a voice blurted out.

It was my other roommate, Jessica Vonn. Jessica was a black girl from Richmond, Virginia. This was her last year in college, so she had her finger on the pulse of everything going on around this campus. She came from a middle-class family. Her dad inherited a funeral home and cremation center after her grandfather died five years ago, according to Jessica. She said she hated it in the beginning when she had to go clean up there after work hours. The stories she told me were quite funny. She didn't think so at first. Luckily for her, she's gotten used to it, so it doesn't bother her that much now.

"A weird girl that lives on the top floor named Penny."

"What about her?" Jessica went into question mode while she took off her shoes and jacket.

"I was just telling Gia how bizarre she was acting when she walked up on me while I was looking at the flyer about the missing girl," I began to explain.

"What did she say?" Jessica wanted to know.

Gia chuckled. "She was being a little stalkerish and creeped her out."

"She told me that every time I enter a room, she hears when girls talk about how pretty and popular I am. And the guys gawk at me and talk about how much they want to be with me. So, in my mind, I'm trying to figure out, how is she hearing all of this? She said more stuff, but I'll be here all night rehashing it."

"Don't pay her any mind. Everybody knows how crazy she is," Jessica insisted.

Agreeing with Jessica, I left that matter alone and changed the subject. "So you heard about the missing girl too?" I asked her.

"Everybody's heard about it," Jessica said.

"Not me. I just found out about her an hour ago."

"Where have you been?" Jessica tossed a question back.

"On campus like everyone else."

"Doesn't seem like it to me," she added, then grabbed a towel, bath cloth, and her robe from her locker. "I'll be back." She smiled and left the room.

"You two are the most cynical chicks I know," I said, nodding.

"But I thought your bestie Maria was?" Gia said sarcastically, and then she smiled.

I threw my pillow at her, and then I looked up at the ceiling and shook my head. "God please help me with these girls."

Dirty Deeds

I couldn't believe how fast spring break arrived. My flight was easy, and I couldn't wait to see my stepfather. I was shocked when I exited the airport and saw my mom's pearl-white late-model Mercedes-Benz parked alongside the curb waiting for me. Mercedes-Benz has always been her thing. I honestly can't remember if she ever drove or owned any other car. See, my mother was a kept chick. I can't say who she was with before my father, but I do know that he took care of her. Her only job was to take care of me and make sure that our housekeeper, our cook, and my nanny did what they were getting paid to do.

We went through a couple of housekeepers and cooks, but somehow my nanny Maggie managed to stay with us until I turned fifteen. Maggie was cool too. She would let me do things that my mom would've never approved of. Back then, she was the best adult friend that I had. Fast-forward to now, my best friend was Maria, and she was in Miami chilling with her family.

"So, what do you want to do while I'm here?" I started off

saying. We had just left LaGuardia Airport and were now five minutes into the drive.

"I didn't plan anything. I put Sydney in charge of all that," she replied very nonchalantly.

"Well, what did he tell you?" I probed.

"I think he said something about taking you shopping. Maybe take a drive to Niagara Falls. See one of those Broadway shows. You know he loves them."

"You know, I'm down for the shopping spree and Niagara Falls, but he can keep that Broadway show. I'll rather go to a movie."

"See, that's what's wrong with you. Have some appreciation and class."

"I have class. And I'm appreciative too," I replied with sarcasm. I mean, how dare she say that shit to me?

"Well, act like it," she replied, as her voice went up a couple of notches.

"Mom, let's not start. I've been in your presence for only five, ten minutes."

"Start what? All I'm saying is—" she started, but I cut her off midsentence.

"Listen, Mom, can we get to your apartment before you start jumping down my throat? You do this every time we get together."

"Yoshi, that is not true and you know it," my mother spat.

"Mom, you are so critical of me. And it started back when I was nine years old. I remember when my elementary school had an art show event for the kids to show off canvases we designed, and when I had my reveal you didn't clap or cheer me on. You clapped for the other kids in my class but not me. And do you know how that made me feel?"

"I only clapped for the other kids because their art projects looked better."

Hearing her say that my classmates' painted canvases looked

better than mine felt like a punch to the gut. "Wait, did you really just say that their art projects looked better than mine?" I had to question her. I needed to make sure that I heard her correctly.

"Yoshi, you know I'm a straight shooter. I don't care who you are."

"I understand that, Mom, but I am your daughter. I'm your only child, and you treat me like a stranger in the street."

"Yoshi, I've been like this for a long time. And I won't change that for anyone. Not even for my husband. Sydney knows how I am, and he has never tried to change me."

"Who cares about Sydney, Mom!" I yelled. "You got trained like a freaking lap dog," I added.

"Stop yelling in my car. You know better than that," she rebuked me.

I literally wanted to rip her head off and throw it out the passenger side window. That's just how angry she was making me. To calm myself down, I turned my focus to the birds flying by. I thought about how free they looked, flying around in the sky. They acted as if they had not a care in the world, and at that moment, I wished I could trade places.

I elected to remain quiet the rest of the drive to my mother's apartment. A few times, I felt that she was going to break the silence, but being the stubborn woman that she was, she'd cut her tongue out of her mouth to spite her face.

Finally, we arrived at her place, and it seemed like it had taken forever. I couldn't wait to get out of the car. If I had been in her car another minute or two, I probably would've pushed her out of her car and would've told the authorities that she jumped out on her own.

After arriving, she and I took the elevator up to the top floor. On the ride, we continued to remain silent. This didn't bother me. I'm used to her petty antics. She's been this way

for as long as I can remember. Thankfully, Sydney was waiting for me on the other side of the door to their penthouse
apartment. His eyes lit up when he saw me, and he gave me
the biggest hug ever.

"Hi, beautiful!" he greeted me while holding me in a
warm embrace.

"Hi, Sydney." I smiled while looking over his shoulder.
My mother had walked by us and continued down the hallway to her bedroom. A few seconds later, I heard her bedroom door close.

After he let me go, we walked to the kitchen, and I took a
seat on one of the stools at the island in the middle of the
kitchen while Sydney grabbed a beer from the refrigerator.
He offered me one, but I declined the offer.

"So how was your flight?" he started off saying after he
took a gulp from his bottle of beer. He planted his back
against the countertop next to the stove. Sydney was a cool
dude. He was an investment banker and made a lot of
money. His short and chubby stature made him look like a
teddy bear. It didn't matter to my mother that he was a
chunky guy, because he had an attractive face and he was
a good man. He spoiled her and she loved it.

"My flight was good. I fell asleep fifteen minutes after the
plane took off," I finally answered.

"So how long will you be here?"

"Until spring break is over. All my friends and dorm buddies flew back home to see their parents, too, and they're
going to stay home until our spring break is over."

"How are your grades?" His questions continued after he
took another mouthful of beer.

"I'm doing great. I had to take an exam right before I left
and passed it with flying colors," I lied.

"That's awesome, Yoshi. So are you dating anyone right
now?"

I smiled bashfully. "Really, Sydney?!"

"What do you mean *really*? And what's up with this Sydney business? I told you to call me Dad," he chastised me in a loving way and then drank more beer from his bottle.

"I know . . ." I started off saying, because he was right. Even though it had only been a few years since my dad passed away, Sydney earned that privilege. He was a good man.

"Are you going to answer my question or what?"

I giggled. "Which one?"

"Oh, okay, I see what you're doing."

"What am I doing?" I smiled.

"You won't tell me who you're dating and you won't call me Dad. But it's okay."

"Stop being a big baby. You know I've got mad love for you," I assured him.

"I know you do," he agreed, and took another drink.

"Are we still going out for dinner this evening?" my mother asked Sydney as she walked into the kitchen. She was wearing a different set of clothes. When she picked me up from the airport, she was wearing a black and white Chanel sweatsuit with a pair of Chanel sneakers to match. Now she was wearing a casual sky-blue, button-down Chanel oxford shirt with a white Chanel tennis skirt. I looked down to her feet and saw that she was wearing a pair of knitted Chanel espadrilles. She looked very fashionable.

"That's the plan," Sydney replied, and then he finished his beer.

"You look cute," I complimented her.

She gave me a half smile. "Thank you."

"Are you about to go somewhere now?" he asked her after he put the empty bottle in the nearby trash bin.

"Yes, I'm gonna run up to the Saks Fifth Avenue in Manhattan. My personal stylist has some new things for me, so I'm going to go and check them out," she explained.

"Why don't you go with her, Yoshi," Sydney suggested.

I looked at him, and then I looked at my mother. I searched her face for any indication that she didn't want me to tag along. Her facial expression was blank. I couldn't read her if my life depended on it. So I allowed her to make the decision about whether she wanted me to go with her.

"Do you want to go?" she finally asked me.

"Sure. But let me use the bathroom first," I told her.

"I'll be waiting."

I got up from the stool and headed to the guest bathroom, which was only ten feet away. So, while using it, I heard my mother and Sydney talking. At first, I couldn't make out what they were saying because my mother spoke in a very low tone. But I heard Sydney clearly.

"It feels really good to have her here," he started off.

I heard my mother sigh, but I heard nothing after that. Just mumbling.

"Are you gonna have that talk with her?" Sydney asked.

"I haven't decided yet," I heard her say barely. Those words piqued my curiosity. What were they talking about? And why were they being so secretive?

"If you decide not to do it now, then try to build up the courage to tell her before she leaves," he continued. I couldn't hear her response. So it seemed like she might've given him a head nod or didn't respond at all.

"Do you know how long you two are going to be out?" He changed the subject.

Once again, I couldn't hear her, so I did what I came in the bathroom to do and then I returned to the kitchen. I smiled at them both. "I'm ready," I announced.

"Let me get my purse and then we'll leave," she said.

"Try not to spend all my money," he joked.

"I'm not the one you should be worrying about," I replied, and then I winked at him.

"Ready?" my mother asked me.

"Yep, I'm ready," I replied.

Sydney walked us to the front door and planted a kiss on my mother's cheek. I thought the gesture was really cute. I could tell how much Sydney loved her.

"Sydney really loves you." I sparked a conversation as we got on the elevator, which was only a few feet away from the door to her penthouse.

"Yeah, he's a good guy," she agreed while we watched the elevator door close.

"I'm sorry about how I talked to you earlier," I apologized. I hoped that by apologizing to her, she would become vulnerable and get up the nerve to talk about the matter she was hiding from me.

"I appreciate you saying that," she responded. And then the elevator door opened. We were on the tenth floor, and in came an elderly white woman. She had to be at least seventy years old. She had the looks and poise of Queen Elizabeth. She dressed like her too. She spoke to us as soon as she looked at the panel and saw that we were going to the first-floor lobby.

"How are you ladies?" she greeted us.

"Fine," I spoke first.

"Great! And you?" my mother chimed in.

"I've never felt better. On my way to have tea and cookies with my daughter. She's waiting for me outside."

"Sounds like fun," I commented.

"Oh, it is. We have our lunch dates at least twice a month. She just got her doctorate degree in medicine. She's an anesthesiologist, and she's always on call. So I try to spend as much time as I can with her while I can."

"That's nice," I said.

"Are you two mother and daughter?"

"Yes, ma'am, we are," my mother answered.

"Are you in college, young lady?"

"Yes," I replied.

"Are you going to school here in New York?"

"No. I'm studying at Old Dominion University in Norfolk, Virginia."

"What's your major?"

"Political science right now. But I'm pursuing a law degree. I'm gonna come back to New York to do that."

"Well, I wish you the best, young lady," she said as the elevator door opened. "Try to spend as much time as you can with your mother. Because you're gonna look back and wonder where that time went. Now, you two ladies take care of yourselves."

"You do the same," my mother said.

"Bye," I added.

The mall was moderately packed. The percentage of women shoppers was higher than the men I saw. I saw a lot of young women too. The pink, blue, and red hair color and butt implants were a telltale sign that they were strippers. I thought about the way they were dressed, how their low-cut tops and tight jeans showed off their bodies. How they changed the way they looked to stand out. It didn't help that my mother noticed three of them strutting with their silicone breast implants and colorful wigs; she had a lot to say about them. Her facial expression was appalling.

"Are you seeing what I am seeing?" she asked me.

"Yep," I replied as we walked beside each other.

"They look like circus clowns."

I chuckled loud enough so that only she could hear me, because I didn't want to draw any attention to us. She wasn't equipped to help me fight off all three girls if they decided to attack us for talking negatively about them.

"If you ever come home looking like that, I'm admitting you to a mental hospital."

I laughed because I knew that she meant it.

When we walked into Saks Fifth Avenue, we met up with her personal shopper, a young white woman named Rainbow. She looked to be in her late twenties. She was a cute, bubbly soul walking around the women's department looking to assist anyone with a limitless credit card.

She smiled boldly when my mom appeared. "Hi there, beautiful," she said as she greeted my mother. They embraced. Then my mom stood to the side and introduced me.

"This is my daughter, Yoshi. Remember I told you that she was spending spring break with Sydney and me?"

"Yes, I remember. How are you, Yoshi?" Rainbow said.

"I'm good. Thank you," I replied.

"Are we shopping for her today too?" she asked my mother.

"If she sees something she wants, she can have it," my mother told her.

Rainbow smiled. "Well, let's start shopping," she said, and led us to the section of the women's department where she had clothes put away for my mom. We sat in chairs next to the changing room and allowed Rainbow to put all the clothes she chose for my mother on display. I think my mom enjoyed this more than Rainbow. She was in her element. Being the wife of a wealthy man, being able to buy expensive things, and being catered to. I had no sense of style until I started watching my mother dress up in her designer duds. I love high fashion and have a few cute handbags, coats, and shoes, but they stayed in my closet at home while I was in college.

"See anything you like?" Mom asked me after Rainbow handed her a glass of champagne.

"Not really. I mean, when am I going to wear it? I'm in class all day, every day," I replied.

"Just get something and wear it while you're here. Those pants and sweatshirt are hideous." She talked down to me.

"They aren't hideous to me," I said sarcastically.

"What do you think, Rainbow? Shouldn't she get a few of those pieces that you have on the rack? I mean, look at what she has on now. How does she expect to find a potential prospect for a husband dressed like this?" My mother pointed at me.

I was so fucking pissed at her I didn't know what to say. Why embarrass me like this? I wasn't looking for a husband. At least let me get out of school first before trying to find a suitable mate. "I am not you, Mom. So stop trying to push a circle into a square hole," I told her as respectfully as I could muster up.

"Please don't embarrass me," she instructed after looking at Rainbow, who was standing next to us.

"Let me leave you two alone for a bit," Rainbow insisted, and then she stepped away.

"What is your problem? You know that I don't tolerate that kind of behavior. And especially in public," she chastised me.

"What about the way you talk to me?" I shot back at her. "Every time I do something that you don't approve of, you always strike it down. I can't seem to do anything right, and I am tired of you treating me that way," I added.

"Yoshi, you're an adult now, so suck it up," she scolded me.

"I don't have time to deal with this mess," I said, and then I got up from the chair and stormed off. I didn't look back.

I walked around the mall for about fifteen minutes, and that's when I decided to take a taxi back to her penthouse. During the ride, she called me a couple of times, but I refused to answer her.

When I returned to the apartment, Sydney was on the phone with her. "She's here now," he told her, holding the receiver out so I could hear.

"I'm on my way," she announced, and the call ended.

"So what happened?" he asked me.

Wishful Thinking

I broke down the entire incident about what happened when my mom and I were in Saks Fifth Avenue. I told him how embarrassed she made me while talking to me in front of Rainbow. "She talked to me like I was some kind of charity case," I said.

"Just give her a chance, Yoshi. She just wants the best for you." He tried to reason her behavior.

"I understand all of that. But I'm an adult now. I don't need her trying to tell me what to do," I expressed.

"Trust me, I agree with everything you're saying. She drives me crazy almost every single day of the week. But I've learned how to deal with it. When she starts telling me what to do, I just tune her out. It's not that hard to do."

"That's you. I'm not doing it," I protested as I sat down on the living room sofa.

"And that's fine. But at the same time, try to figure out a way to coexist while you're here," he advised.

I looked down at the floor and then looked back up. "Does she even love me?" I questioned him after meeting his eyes.

"Of course she does, Yoshi," he answered as he sat down and threw his arms around my shoulders to embrace me. He held me firmly.

"She doesn't act like it. She treats a stranger better than she does me."

Sydney released his hold and tilted me back just enough so that he could look at me face-to-face. "She's just going through a lot right now. So give her a chance."

"I heard you two talking before we left. I heard you ask her if she'd told me anything yet. What is going on? What does she need to tell me?"

Sydney looked at me like a deer in headlights. He was not expecting me to throw that question his way. He sat there like he was at a loss for words.

"Sydney, tell me what's going on? What's the big secret?"

"What are you guys talking about?" my mother asked. She literally came out of nowhere. I didn't hear her come in from the front door. She stood in the entryway of the living room holding her shopping bags.

"Wow, you got here pretty fast," Sydney commented.

I just sat there and looked at her. I honestly didn't have any words for her.

Sydney did, though. He stood up from the sofa and walked toward her. "So what did you get?" he asked her.

"Am I going to get an answer or what?" my mother asked as she looked at me and then turned her attention back toward Sydney.

"Look, this is not my battle. I'm going to excuse myself and let you two handle this." Sydney left the room.

I got up from the sofa and followed Sydney.

"And where are you going?" she said calmly.

"I really don't have any words right now," I told her as I continued to walk behind Sydney.

"Yoshi, don't walk away from me while I am talking to you."

"But I don't have anything to say."

"Well, you just stand there while I say what I've got to say."

I stopped in my tracks and turned around toward her. I did this because I felt in my gut that she was about to apologize to me. And I needed to hear it.

She walked toward me after she dropped her shopping bags on the floor near the wall. As she came within ten feet of me, she gave me a stern look and said, "Get rid of this temper tantrum, because you're not a baby. I raised you to have thick skin, so this should be nothing new. You're a strong young lady, so act like it."

"Do you know that I only went to school down south to get away from you?" I said, hoping that I was going to hit a nerve with my words. "I could've gone to any of these universities here in New York, but I refused to apply to them. There was no way in hell that I was going to allow you to be within driving distance of me."

"Oh really?" She put her hand on her left hip.

"Yeah, really. And so you know, Sydney and I were talking about you. I asked him why you were so mean to me, and you know what he said? He told me to give you a chance because you're going through something and that you really love me."

"So he had to tell you that I love you for you to believe it?"

"Whether I believe it or not, you suck as a mother. And—" I was cut off as she lunged forward and slapped the hell out of me. The slap had so much power that it almost caused me to collapse onto the floor.

I cradled my cheek with the palm of my hand. "What the fuck is wrong with you? You can't just walk around and slap people when you want to!" I roared. I swear, I was two seconds away from hitting her ass back.

Luckily for her, Sydney came running down the hallway. "What's going on?" he asked us both.

I walked away from them and went to my bedroom. I slammed the door shut and then locked it so I couldn't have any unwanted guests. My mother in particular.

I heard my mom trying to explain what transpired before she hit me. The version of her story made it seem like I was asking for her to put her hands on me.

"Sydney, I'm not allowing a child of mine to come into my house and disrespect me. She needs to count her blessings, because I could've hit her harder."

"Look, babe, I understand how you feel about children disrespecting their parents, but you could've handled this a little differently."

"Oh, so now you're taking her side? I knew that her coming here for two weeks would be too much for me to handle." I could tell that Sydney was about to be on her shit list. She hates when someone goes against her.

"No, baby, I'm not. And come on, why would you say that?" He tried to calm the situation down.

"Don't act like you're just now hearing this. You know that she and I don't get along. Oh but, to let you tell it, everything is going to run smoothly. She and I are going to bridge the gap from all the conflicts that we've had in the past. But just as I thought, shit will fall apart, and that's what happened."

"Please do this for me. You two need to come together."

"The only way I'll even contemplate talking to her is if she apologizes to me. No child of mine will stand in my house and talk to me like that." She continued yapping her mouth. I was becoming more furious with each second. My mind was spinning in a circular motion. It felt as if her words were slamming against my head. I knew then that it was time for me to get out of this house before I say something else to her that would convince her that I disrespected her.

I grabbed my suitcase and duffle bag. I opened my bedroom door with apprehension, because I knew that as soon as she saw me, she was going to have more words for me and I didn't have the energy for it. I thought my mom and Sydney were still in the hallway, but as they continued to talk, I realized that they were in their bedroom. This was the perfect time for me to make my exit.

With every step I took, the words from my mother and Sydney became fainter.

"Will you calm down, please? She's here and we're gonna make the best of this trip." was the last thing I heard before I opened the front door and closed it behind me.

No one interrupted my elevator ride on the way down to the first-floor lobby, so I was relieved by that. Upon exiting the front door of the lobby, I noticed that my taxi driver was waiting curbside for me. When he realized I was his customer, he got out of his car and helped me put my things in his car. "Is someone else coming?" he asked after we got in the taxi.

"Nope, it's just me," I told him, and watched as he drove away from the valet area of the apartment building.

"The sun went down really fast. I just left the mall and went into the penthouse less than an hour ago," I said.

"I've been out all day, so I haven't noticed it," the driver replied. He was a young black guy who looked like he wasn't a day over twenty. He resembled the singer Johnny Gill and had a heavy New York accent. "So you're going to the Sheraton next to the airport?"

I inhaled and exhaled. "Yep. I just left my mother's apartment. I'm on spring break and was supposed to spend that time with my mother, but she screwed it up. I just flew in this morning from Virginia, and now I'm about to stay at the Sheraton overnight and then take a flight out of here to-morrow."

"Don't do that. You haven't even been here for twenty-four hours. Why don't you just sleep on it for the night and then call her in the morning? And who knows, she may think about what transpired between you two and want to apologize," he reasoned.

I chuckled. "If only you knew," I commented, and I turned my attention toward the cars riding alongside of us.

"Have you prayed about it?"

Shocked by his question, I turned my attention back to him. He was looking at me in his rearview mirror.

"No, I haven't," I answered.

"Do you go to church?"

"No."

"What about your mother?"

"No."

"Did you go to church as a child?"

"Two or three times with my dad."

"Have you been saved?"

"No disrespect, but you are asking me too many questions right now," I said. I had too much shit on my plate to be in his therapy session.

"I'm sorry about that. But can I say one more thing?"

I hesitated for a moment, and then I gave him the green light. "Don't make it too long," I instructed him.

"I just wanna say that God is your answer. He will fix everything in your life that's broken. I'm a witness to that," he replied, and then he fell silent.

He didn't say one word to me the entire drive to the Sheraton hotel. But guess what? I thought about everything he said. I know God is real and he'll handle every situation that comes your way. But he takes too long to work out things in a person's life. I want my situations to be resolved as soon as they happen. I guess it would have been a good time to ask God to give me some patience.

As soon as we arrived at the hotel, my driver grabbed my luggage and handed the bags to me right after I got out of the car. He smiled at me and said, "Hope you remember what I said."

I smiled. "I will, don't worry. And I'm truly sorry for being a butthole."

"It's okay to have a bad day. Just don't have too many of them."

"Pray for me, please."

"I will, and don't *you* worry," he assured me, and then he got back in his car.

Keep Your Apologies to Yourself

Sydney figured out that I had left the house while I was checking into my hotel room. He called every bit of ten times before realizing that I wasn't going to answer his call. Sydney was a good guy, so I felt bad not answering his phone call because of something my mother did. My mother always finds a way to put him in the middle of our bullshit!

After calling American Airlines, I finally found a flight leaving New York at six twenty-five in the morning. I left a message for my roommates, telling them the change in plans and how to reach me.

Since I hadn't eaten much, I decided to get me some room service. I ordered a cheeseburger with everything on it and a side of French fries, and boy was it good. I topped my delicious sandwich down with a cold Sprite. I swear, it felt like I was in heaven, especially when I lay in my bed, stuffed inside these sofa sheets and fluffy comfortable. The Sheraton sure knows how to treat a girl.

I tried to go to sleep, but my mind wouldn't let me. The argument I had with my mother was weighing heavily on my mind. For the life of me, I couldn't figure out why she hated me. She's a fucking bitch, and I couldn't believe how Sydney could live under the same roof. That bitch would make me crazy.

I started sifting through channels in hopes of finding something that I could watch until I fell asleep. Unfortunately for me, nothing on the local channels interested me, so I ordered a movie. It was called *Child's Play*. I saw the first part over a year ago and loved it, so there was no doubt in my mind that this installment would be good.

Twenty minutes into the film, the room phone started ringing; I ignored it because I knew that it was either my mom or Sydney. The phone rang five times and then stopped. Two minutes passed, and then the phone started ringing again. This time it rang six times and then it went to the answering machine. "Sorry we're unavailable to take your call. Please leave a message after the tone."

"This message is for Yoshi. My name is Jessica. I'm Yoshi's other roommate. Would you please tell her to call me back at the dorm? It's about our roommate Gia. Thank you." After hearing the urgency in Jessica's message, I was struck with a sharp pain in my gut, but I snapped out of it. I jumped up, raced over to the telephone, and called her back.

She answered the dorm room phone on the first ring. "Hello," she said. She sounded so distraught that her voice was cracking.

"Jessica, what happened?" I asked her.

"Gia overdosed and now she's at the hospital," she said between sniffles.

"When did this happen? And what hospital is she at?"

"This happened like an hour ago. My friend Poppi called me and asked me where I was, because she saw paramedics go to my room. I was at the library at the time and told her that when I left the room, Gia was there. So I ran back to the dorm, and when I got there I saw the paramedics taking her out on a stretcher with an oxygen mask covering her face. I almost lost it right there."

"How do you know that she OD'd?"

"Because that what everybody on our floor said. They heard the paramedics say it."

"Where are you now?"

"At the hospital."

"Well, I'm gonna fly out tomorrow morning."

"No, wait, I didn't call you to take you from your family. I just wanted you to know what was going on."

"Don't worry about my family. I'm at a hotel now because me and my mother got into an argument. I booked a flight to leave here in the morning, so as soon as I arrive back in Norfolk, I'll call you."

"Okay."

"Hey, wait, has anyone talked to her parents?"

"Yes, I heard that they were en route."

"All right, I'll see you in the morning. Stay calm and try to keep a level head. She's gonna be all right." I tried to console her.

"I'll try." It was all she could say, and then she ended the call.

Sick to my stomach and with an uncontrollable heartbeat, I sat up in the bed and wished that I wasn't there. I'd known my trip home for spring break was going to be a disaster before I called American Airlines to purchase the ticket over a month ago. Now I was regretting that I hadn't been at school to prevent my roommate from doing that to herself. I knew all I could do was wait until morning and get out of here.

Too Close to Home

I finally caught a couple of Zzz's. The last time I looked at the digital clock on the nightstand, it said 1:18 a.m. Now it said 4:10, which meant that I had only three hours of sleep. But that meant nothing to me, because I had to get back to Norfolk so I could check on Gia. While I was packing my things to go to the airport, I noticed that Sydney hadn't called, and I was good with that. I hated having him in the middle of my mother's bullshit! She's an asshole in every sense of the word.

I arrived at the airport an hour earlier than my flight. It didn't matter that I had to wait to board my plane. Just the thought of leaving New York to go back to Norfolk to check on Gia made me feel better.

Thankfully my flight landed on time. So as soon as I stepped foot into the airport, I made a run to the baggage claim area. I was the first one there from my flight. Unfortunately, my suitcase was one of the last that came in. It was OK, though. I just wanted to get out of there so I could go to the hospital to check on my friend.

With my luggage in hand, I caught a taxi straight to the hospital. While en route, I couldn't help but think about Gia's condition. I hoped that it was just something minor and that she'd come out fine.

I couldn't believe how fast my taxi driver got me to the hospital. Within minutes, I was in the hospital lobby, then on the elevator and at the intensive care floor. I saw Jessica as soon as I turned the corner from one hallway to the next. There was a guy sitting next to her. I started walking fast until we were face-to-face. I called out her name low enough so that only she could hear it. When she turned her attention toward me, her face and eyes were red and puffy. My heart went out to her. She got up from her chair and came toward me. We came together and braced each other. "She's in a coma. She may not wake back up." Jessica sobbed near my shoulders.

"No, don't talk like that. She's going to be fine. We've got to speak life and her," I instructed Jessica. "How many family members in her room?"

"Four people. Her mother, her dad, her sister, and her grandmother," Jessica replied between the sniffles.

"Who is that guy sitting next to you?"

"Her brother."

"Has he been in there to see her?"

"Yeah, just came out because only four people can be in there at a time."

"How long has she been in a coma?"

"Right after she got here. It's medically induced. If they bring her out, she'll die within an hour." Jessica continued to cry. By this time my shirt was drenched with her tears. But it didn't matter. Jessica was like family to me. Gia too. We looked out for one another, through the good and the bad.

"Has her family sat down and talked to you?" I asked her

after I walked her farther away from Gia's room and the brother.

Jessica looked over her shoulder and then turned her attention back toward me. "I didn't see them until late last night. And after they spoke to the doctors, they pulled me to the side and grilled me. They wanted to know where I was when Gia overdosed. I told them I was at the library. So they asked me if I knew Gia was on drugs. What kind of drugs she was taking. How often she got high. Who she got high with. And they even asked me who she was getting the drugs from. Her dad said that if he finds out who sold her the drugs, he's going to hurt them badly and then let the cops arrest them."

Hearing Jessica's words immediately gave me anxiety because I knew that they were going to question me like they did Jessica. What was I going to do? I didn't sell her the drugs, but I knew how often she got high and I knew where she got her drugs. "How long have they been in the room?" I wanted to know.

"I don't know, maybe thirty to forty minutes."

"Come on, let's go to the lounge. I'm not ready to see her parents right now," I stated, and grabbed Jessica's hand. I escorted her down two hallways that led to one of the hospital's family lounges.

Fortunately, no one was in the lounge, so Jessica and I had some privacy. We took a seat near the clear glass window so we could see when someone was coming our way. "Seen any cops snooping around and asking questions?" I asked her.

"Not yet. But I saw a couple of them walking around our dorm, asking the other girls questions."

"What about the teaching staff or faculty? Have they been asking questions?"

"I heard they've been to the dorm asking questions too. But I've been here since the paramedics brought Gia here."

"Did you do a sweep on our room? You know that we could be kicked out of school if they found something."

"Yeah, I cleaned it."

"Has her brother talked to you?"

"No, he hasn't said one word. He lets his parents do all the talking."

"Damn, Jessica! I can't believe this is happening. Something told me not to leave," I said, and then I paused. "If I was here, this would not have happened," I continued while blaming myself. And at that moment, I started sobbing too. I buried my face in the palms of my hands. "God, please don't let her die. She's a good person," I cried. Jessica embraced me.

"We've got to stay strong for her," Jessica reminded me as she rubbed my back in a circular motion.

"This can't be real," I commented, and then I got up from the chair. I walked to the doorway and peered around it. I wanted to make sure none of Gia's family was coming in our direction. When I saw that the coast was clear, I went back and sat down next to Jessica. "We've gotta come up with a good-ass story about Gia's drug use. Because if we don't, shit will hit the fan and we're going to feel every drop of that shit."

Although Jessica felt like she was out of the woods because she answered all of Gia's parents' questions, I knew better. To find out that your daughter was in the hospital and on her deathbed stirs a lot of things in your mind. I knew that if I had a daughter, I wouldn't stop asking questions until I felt like I'd heard all I needed to know.

Jessica and I sat in the lounge for at least twenty minutes trying to figure out what we were going to do about the situation, as we were Gia's closest friends. For God's sake, we did everything together.

While mulling over various stories to tell her family, Jessica and I heard the footfalls of two people coming our way. We stopped talking and listened. My heart skipped a beat, and I was sure Jessica's did as well because of the way she looked at me. As soon as we both blinked, the steps got closer and then two people appeared.

"Lisa. Chelsea," I said. It was a relief knowing that they were people we knew other than Gia's family. I waved at them both while Jessica stood up to greet them. They embraced Jessica and asked her about Gia's condition.

"So what's going on?"

"Yeah, where is she?"

"They got her in one of the rooms in the intensive care unit. Her mom and her dad are in the room with her. Her brother is sitting outside the room waiting to get his turn," Jessica explained.

"Have you gotten a chance to see her?" Chelsea asked, standing in the middle of the room.

"Yeah, Jessica, how does she look?"

"I saw her only briefly, because I couldn't stand there and watch her with all that medical equipment they have connected to her."

"Does she look the same?" Chelsea wanted to know.

"Yeah. Does she look the same?" Lisa chimed in.

"Yes, she does. Thank God," Jessica answered.

"Have you guys talked to their parents?" Lisa asked.

"I talked to them. But they haven't seen Yoshi yet," Jessica replied.

"Have the cops come here yet?" Chelsea started. "They've been asking a lot of questions back at the dorm. Whoever knows Gia, they've talked to them."

"Who have they talked to?" I asked her.

"I saw them talk to Bridget, Samantha, and I think Michelle," Chelsea replied.

"What kind of questions did they ask them?" I wanted to know.

"Yeah, what did they say?" Jessica asked.

"I don't know what they asked them, but they asked me, How long have you known Gia? Who are her roommates? Do I know whether she has a drug habit? If so, how long? What kinds of people does she roommate with? Are you a drug user too? If so, what kind of drugs do you use? How often? I mean, the list goes on and on. They were grilling me like I did something wrong," Chelsea explained.

"What did you tell them?" I interjected.

"I basically said that I've known her since she's been going to school here. I told them that she and I do homework together sometimes. I told them overall that she's a good girl. And that I didn't know she had a drug habit. But I don't think they believed me," Chelsea continued.

"Why you say that?" I asked.

"Because they said I spent too much time with her not to know that she uses drugs. But I stuck to my story," Chelsea added.

"What did you tell him about me and Jessica?"

"I told him that I knew you guys around the same amount of time as I knew Gia and if anyone knew about Gia having a drug addiction, you two would know."

"Why would you say something like that? Now they're going to be breathing down our necks for answers that we can't even give them," I exploded.

"Yeah, Chelsea, that was a fucked-up move. I mean, you should've just said that you didn't know. Now the cops and her parents are going to be looking at me sideways. I don't need that type of heat in my life right now. I've got too much shit on my plate as it is," Jessica responded sarcastically.

"You guys just need to calm down. Gia wouldn't want us acting like this with each other," Lisa chimed in, attempting to defuse the situation.

When Lisa interjected, I turned my attention to her and asked what the cops had asked her. Like dominoes, Jessica and Chelsea turned their attention toward Lisa, and I waited for her answer.

"They pretty much asked me the same questions," she replied.

"And what did you say to them?" Jessica wanted to know.

"I said that I've known Gia for a little over a year and that we had a couple of classes together. I told them that I kind of suspected her taking a couple of Mollys every now and again, just to eliminate the pressure of doing well in her classes. They asked me if she had a boyfriend, and I told him that she did have one but they broke up like five to six months ago. Then they asked me how well I knew you two. And I told them that I really didn't know much about you or Jessica, so I couldn't make an assumption about whether you knew that Gia was getting high . . ."

"Hello, ladies," said a male voice.

Surprised by the sudden interruption, everyone in the lounge looked at the entryway. A Hispanic detective was standing at the doorway, and next to him was Gia's brother. It was evident to me that he was showing the cop where we were, because after he pointed toward us, he walked off in the opposite direction.

I knew the cop was a detective at first glance because he wasn't in a police-issued uniform. He was a slender, medium height, average-looking cop. He wore casual dark blue pants, a jacket, and a button-down collar shirt. He also wore a sporty pair of black sunglasses.

"Hello," Chelsea replied.

Jessica, Lisa, and I gave him a quick acknowledgment with our hands. "Did I interrupt anything?" he asked as he approached us.

"No, not really," Jessica spoke up.

"I remember speaking to you ladies last night," he announced after he got within arm's reach of us. "I spoke to you too," he said to Jessica after jogging his memory. "So who are you?" he asked me while he grabbed a little notebook from the inside of his jacket pocket.

"My name is Yoshi. I was in New York when all of this took place," I started off saying.

"Oh, so you're the other roommate?"

"Yes."

"Ladies, mind if I talk to her alone?" And when he uttered those words, I was about to shit in my pants. Not knowing the questions he was going to ask me gave me a ball of nerves in the pit of my stomach. I could just get up and walk away, but I knew that would make it seem like I was hiding something, so I sat there.

After he shook my hand and identified himself as Detective Louis, he had his pen and paper ready to write down everything I was about to say.

"What's your full name?"

"Yoshi Lomax," I replied.

"Nice name," he complimented.

"Thank you."

"How well do you know Gia?"

"I know her pretty well. But that doesn't mean that she tells me everything."

"How long have you two been roommates?"

"Close to two years."

"Does she have a boyfriend?"

"She sees guys here and there, but that's it."

"How is her emotional state of mind?"

"I can't say. I'm not a doctor."

"Well, then tell me, has she been depressed lately?"

"If she has been, then I don't know about it," I lied. I knew Gia was depressed. Her boyfriend broke up with her months ago for no reason, and it's been hard for her to move on.

"Did you know that she was using drugs?"

I hesitated for a second because I knew that whatever I said would be used against me at a later date. Oh, also I knew that when you lie, you'll have to come up with another lie to cover for that. So what do I say? Do I tell them the truth? Or should I lie?

"It's OK, you can tell me," the cop pressed.

"Hey look, sir, you and I both know that drugs are illegal. Our school prohibits the use of drugs. She was brought here because of a drug overdose. And if they find out that a student is a drug user, then that's automatic grounds for dismissal. So how should I answer your question?" I questioned him.

"Are you stating these facts because you use drugs?"

"I have from time to time, especially around exam time."

"What kind of drugs have you used?"

"Nothing too hard. Marijuana," I lied. I had to give them the name of a recreational drug just in case the dean of ODU started asking more detailed questions. At least then, if I was thrown into the mix, I could walk away with only a slap on the wrist and ordered academic probation by doing all my classes online for a whole semester. But if I told them that I used any other potent prescription drug, they would know that I knew about Gia's addiction and we got high together, and then I'd be kicked out of school. Gia can already kiss her studies here good-bye, because if she pulled out of this, she would be expelled.

"Are you being up-front with me?" he nudged me, probably thinking that I was going to change my story. Did he think I was stupid?

"Yes," I said. But just like Jessica said, he wasn't buying our shit. He knew that we were lying through our teeth. But I couldn't change my story, because they'd open the floodgates. He'd ask me who our drug dealer was. How much drugs did we buy? How often do we buy? I wasn't putting my business out there like that. There were plenty of jealous girls around campus who would have loved to hear about what went on behind the door of our dorm room.

"Does your other roommate, Jessica, use drugs?" He turned the question around, hoping that I'd rat her out.

"Not to my knowledge."

"Come on, now, you can be candid with me. She already told me that she'll pop a pill or two when she needs to relax."

"Well, if that's what she said, then go off of that," I answered, but he knew that I was lying.

"Who do you purchase your marijuana from?"

"I don't know the guy's name."

"Why not? Everybody knows who their dealer is. If you don't know his real name, then he goes by a nickname."

"I don't get my marijuana from the same guy. I get it from whoever is around. I give them the money, and they give me the weed. And then we go our separate ways."

"You're a hard cookie to crumble," he commented.

"That's because I'm not a cookie," I responded nonchalantly.

"What's your major?"

"Political science."

"Oh, so you're interested in politics, huh?"

"Yep." I gave him a one-word answer.

"Is that why you only smoke weed?"

"Yep." I gave him another one-word answer.

"How will it affect you if she doesn't come out of that coma?"

"What kind of question is that? It would devastate me."

"Well, if it would devastate you, then why aren't you being transparent with me? Tell what you girls really do in that dorm room," he probed.

"We do what any other girls would do in their dorm room."

"What kind of stuff?" He wouldn't let up.

"Stuff that girls do."

"Can you give me an example?"

"We do our school work together. Eat. Talk shit about guys. You know the girl stuff."

"What about drugs? Did you guys get high together?"

"I told you that I don't know about any drug use."

"Yes."

"Well then, that means that we didn't get high together," I pointed out to him.

Before the detective could ask me another question, Gia's mother appeared. She stormed into the lounge and went straight into question mode. "I need some answers," she said without hesitation.

She was bawling, and her face was flushed. She looked like she'd been crying all morning.

"Mrs. Santos, I'm trying to conduct an interview. I'll let you speak with her in a moment," the cop insisted.

"I've been calling her since late last night, so what I need to say won't take long," Gia's mother insisted.

Puzzled by her remark, I spoke up. "I haven't gotten a call from you. When did you try to call me?"

"Jessica gave me your number last night around nine, so I called you immediately thereafter," she told me.

"She must've given you the wrong number, because the only call I got last night was from Jessica and that's it."

"Mrs. Santos, please give me a moment to finish my interview and then you can have her," he promised. He was getting irritated. But she wasn't backing down.

She folded her arms against her chest and stood there. "Well, I'm gonna stand right here until you're done," she insisted.

"I can't allow you to do that," he informed her. "But I'll tell you what, if you step outside this room and close the door behind you, I would be grateful."

Mrs. Santos was very reluctant to move, and the detective

knew this. "Ma'am, just give me two more minutes and then you can have her," he added, and that's when she turned around and left the room. The detective closed the door after she walked across the threshold. When he turned around, he started grilling me again.

"Who is responsible for giving Gia drugs? Now, before you answer, think about Gia. If she doesn't come out of that coma, her blood will be on your hands," he warned me.

"I don't know." I stuck to my guns. I was not taking the blame for Gia's situation. And I wasn't going to rat out Rita Reznik either. I heard rumors about how notorious and deadly her father was. He had the reputation of being very dangerous, so their names would never come out of my mouth, especially to a cop.

"I think you do. I spoke with a dorm resident, and she told me that Gia's drug supplier is your marijuana supplier."

"Well, if she said that, then why didn't she give you his or her name?" I responded sarcastically.

"She did. I just wanted you to confirm what she said."

Out of frustration, I sucked my teeth. "Look, I don't have time for this. No one in my dorm told you shit, because if they did, then you'd be arresting Gia's supplier right now. But instead, you wanna harass me. I hate what happened to her and I pray that she wakes up, because I love her like a sister. But I'm not her babysitter. So do your job and leave me alone," I told him, and then I stepped away from him.

"If she doesn't pull through, then you and I will have another discussion," he warned me.

I ignored him. I was getting mentally prepared to have this one-on-one chat with Gia's mom. As soon as I opened the door, she was eyeballing me. She was standing up with her back against the wall, but when I crossed over the threshold, she pushed her weight forward and started walking toward me.

Mrs. Santos was an attractive woman. She had smooth

skin, beautiful hazel eyes, and long natural curly black hair. She was average height and rather thin. But when she opened her mouth, she roared like a lion.

"What did you do to my baby?" she cried out. By this time, she was only three feet away from me.

Detective Louis was standing in the background, at about fifty feet. "Mrs. Santos, we're in ICU, so you gotta bring your volume down," he instructed her.

"Mrs. Santos, I didn't do anything," I replied as meekly as I could. I watched the detective from my peripheral vision, and I could tell that he was waiting for me to say something to incriminate myself. Or be more inclined to answer her question, since I didn't give him the time of day.

"Gia told me months ago that she tried prescription drugs one time at a party with you and some other girl and that it was a one-time thing. She promised me that she wouldn't do it again, so who gave her those drugs?" she asked through gnashing teeth.

Taken aback by her question and declaration, I didn't know what to say. I mean, did Gia really tell her mother that she started popping prescriptions at a party with me and a friend? That threw me for a loop. Why would she do that? This lady was looking at me like I was the reason that Gia was in a coma fighting for her life. Unbeknownst to everyone standing in this hallway, Gia introduced me to prescription drugs, so she needed to do some fact checking. Whether her mom knew it or not, Gia was depressed. Gia always talked about being bullied in middle and high school because she wasn't popular. She wore thick bifocals and hand-me-downs from older cousins in the family. Things got worse when she became a young adult. Not being able to keep a steady boyfriend and getting one-night stands opened the doors for low self-esteem. So she can miss me with that foolishness. Gia was popping pills before we met. She was the one who introduced me to Rita, not the other way around.

"I'm sorry, Mrs. Santos, but Gia could not have told you that, because I don't pop pills. She has a couple more friends that she hangs out with, so maybe you should ask them," I finally answered her.

"But you smoke marijuana, right?" the cop interjected.

I sucked my teeth and rolled my eyes at his goofy-looking ass.

"Oh, so you don't pop pills but you smoke marijuana?" she hissed. I could see proverbial steam from her ears.

"Mrs. Santos, please don't listen to him. I went home to my family's house for spring break, and as soon as I heard about what happened to Gia, I got on a plane and came right back," I tried to explain in a mild way. I really didn't book a flight to come back to Virginia because of Gia's situation, but she didn't need to know it.

"How long has she been on that mess?" Mrs. Santos wanted to know.

"I'm not sure," I lied.

"Who are the other friends that you said she supposedly hung around with?" she pressed me. This lady wasn't letting me breathe. It felt like she had a chokehold on me.

As I opened my mouth to tell Mrs. Santos that I didn't know any of the names of the other girls she hung out with, I saw the detective stand there motionless, awaiting my response. I shut him and Mrs. Santos down. "I don't know the girls by name. I just see them from time to time," I replied, and boy was Mrs. Santos pissed.

"You are a fucking liar! You know every one of the girls my daughter hangs out with. For God's sake, you are her roommate. Do you think I am stupid? You know something and you're trying to hide it. But I will get to the bottom of this," she finished ranting, and then she walked away.

Watching Mrs. Santos as she stormed off in the direction of Gia's room, I knew that I wasn't going to see Gia today while she was here, so I picked my feelings up from the floor and walked in the opposite direction. The detective was still hanging around. "It didn't work out as well as you thought, huh?" he commented. He was being a fucking jerk.

Once again, I ignored him and went on my merry way, even though I wasn't feeling merry. I assumed that after the disastrous chat with Mrs. Santos, the cop would follow me and invade my space, but he didn't. Thank God! Because I was not in the mood to deal with another round of questions.

It was so disturbing that they were treating me like I was the one who gave Gia the fucking drugs. I am not a villain. I'm just a young girl trying to get through school. Go to law school, obtain my law degree, become an attorney, and eventually become a partner at a prestigious law firm. But when I looked around at my immediate surroundings, I saw Mrs. Santos walking down the hallway toward Gia's room and then this detective standing around like a fly on shit. I could see that he was going to be a thorn in my side, so I knew I would have to step my game up and stay off their radar, because shit wouldn't end well if I didn't.

Monkey See, Monkey Do

I took the elevator down to the main entrance of the hospital, and when the elevator door opened, there was Jessica standing before me. The last time I had seen her was when she left the family lounge room so that the detective could interview me. She took a couple of steps backward so I could get off the elevator. "Where are you coming from? I just left you upstairs," I wondered aloud.

"I came down here to get me a soda and Gia a flower arrangement. But I should be asking you where you going?"

"After that conversation I had with Gia's mom and that cop, I decided that I couldn't take it anymore, so I came down here so that I could send for a taxi cab."

"What did they say?" Jessica asked me while she tugged on my arm and pulled me toward a two-seater lounge chair a few feet away from the elevator.

"Mrs. Santos came at me like I gave Gia the drugs. She got in my face and called me a liar. She insinuated that I was the one to have caused Gia to overdose because Gia told her one time that she and I and another girl took her to a party and gave her prescription pills," I explained after sitting down. Jessica sat down next to me.

"Oh yeah, I remember that night. I was with y'all."

"Well, then you're the girl she was talking about. She was bugging out, Jessica. And then I had to deal with that cop, asking me who the supplier was that sold Gia the drugs. And threatening to charge me with a crime if Gia doesn't come out of her coma."

"He can't do that."

"I know that, but his dumb ass doesn't know I know it."

"Think she's gonna pull through this?"

"I hope she does. She's had a lot of issues, but she's a good girl."

"Yeah, she is," Jessica agreed. "So did you get a chance to see Gia?"

"Nope. After that powwow with her mother, I knew that she wasn't going to let me in her room, so I got on the elevator and came down here."

"I'll tell you what, let me take these flowers back upstairs and I'll come right back to take you back to campus."

"You don't have to do that. I can take a taxi."

"Nope. We came here together and we shall leave together. So sit tight and I'll be right back," Jessica assured me, then she got up and began to walk away.

While I watched her cruise toward the elevator, it dawned on me that I needed to call my parents to let them know that I had gotten back to Virginia safely. I called them from the pay phone forty feet from where I was sitting. With no change in hand, I had to place a collect call. After my stepfather answered the phone and accepted, I said, "Hello."

"Hi, Yoshi, I'm glad you called. Where are you? Your mother and I are worried sick about you."

"I'm fine, Dad, I'm back in Virginia."

"Why did you go back? Your mother and I had a lot of fun things planned for you to do."

"Sydney, don't lie for my mother. I heard everything she said after I went to my bedroom. She doesn't like me for some insane reason, and I can't put my finger on it. So the best thing for me to do is stay away from her. She's toxic, and I don't ever see her being anything different."

"She's going through something."

"Sydney, stop making excuses for her behavior. Take her to see a shrink or something. She needs help," I suggested sarcastically.

"I'll tell you what, since you're still on spring break, mind if your mother and I get a flight to come to Virginia and hang out on the beach?"

"As much as I would love to see you, right now isn't a good time. My roommate overdosed last night from drugs, so I'm at the hospital."

"What kind of drugs?"

"Cocaine."

"When you say overdosed, are you saying that she's dead?"

"No. They have her on a ventilator to help her breathe. So, in essence, she's in a medically induced coma."

"No way! My heart goes out to that young lady."

"Me too. But all we can do now is pray for her to recover. She's like a sister to me, so the quicker we can get her back, the better off everyone will be."

"Well, I'll make sure your mother and I pray for her. We're gonna pray for you too."

"Thank you," I said.

He and I talked for a few more minutes until I saw Jessica get off the elevator. As she started walking toward me, I told him that I had to go. Before he and I ended the call, he told me that he and my mother loved me. For what it's worth, I knew he did, but my mother, I don't think so. Maybe one day I'll find out why.

"You didn't have to get off the phone for me," she said.

"It's okay. It wasn't anyone but my stepdad. I was just briefing him on Gia's condition," I told her.

"Wait, so you told him that she OD'd on drugs?"

"Yeah, I told him."

"What did he say?"

"He told me that he and my mom will pray for her."

"Did he ask you whether you were using drugs too?"

"Nope. But if I had that same conversation with my mother, she would've asked me," I stated. "Did you see Gia's mom around when you went back to her room?"

"I saw her pacing around in a circle outside of Gia's room, talking to someone on the phone. At one point, I heard her cry, but it wasn't loud." Jessica told me the details as we exited the hospital.

"Did anyone else from the campus pop up while you were there?"

"No, just the ones you and I talked to before the cop pulled you to the side."

"I sure pray that she pulls through this. It won't be the same if she leaves us. I mean, there's not a person on campus that doesn't like her. She's a cool roommate, and she'll give you the shirt off her back if you ask her."

"I know. I love when we order food together. She'll order the whole damn menu and then pay for all the food," Jessica said as we got into her car, and then she chuckled.

After I closed the passenger side door, I watched her start the ignition, and it prompted me to say, "Think I could get charged if Gia died?"

"What kind of question is that, Yoshi? You and I both know that that fool can't charge you with anything."

"Jessica, the laws change all the time. They could come up with distribution or enabling. You know how the cops are. If they can find a way to charge you, they will do it," I told her as she drove out of the parking lot.

"Yoshi, you didn't do any of those crimes that you just named. You were in freaking New York when she overdosed, so stop bugging out. You're gonna be fine," Jessica promised.

"You better be right," I said, and nudged her arm.

"I will be right. But why are you being paranoid all of a sudden? You study law. You know that he can't charge you with anything."

"You're right. I do know. It's just that when you know something to be a fact, doubt finds a way to creep in the back of your mind and start to make you question yourself."

"Well, get it together. You're gonna be fine and so will I."

After we arrived back on campus, Jessica and I ran into Maria walking across the corridor. I hadn't seen her since we left for spring break, so we hugged each other while Jessica stood there next to me. "I heard what happened to Gia. Are you all right?" she started off saying. Maria wasn't too fond of Gia, so it was weird hearing her voice her concerns for her.

"I'm okay, but Gia overdosed on coke and prescription drugs and now she's in a medically induced coma."

"I'm sorry to hear that," Maria said.

"I appreciate you saying that."

"I know you do, but promise me that the same thing doesn't happen to you."

"What does that mean?" I asked her, but I knew what she was talking about.

"Just keep your nose clean," she replied sarcastically, and then she walked away. "She really hates Gia, huh?" Jessica asked.

"No, it's not like she hates her. She just thinks that Gia isn't a good person to hang around with, especially because she gets high."

"Well, you do it."

"See, that's the thing. She feels like I do it because of Gia."

"She's so judgmental. I see why Gia doesn't like her," Jessica hissed.

I inhaled and exhaled. "I just wish all of you guys would bury the hatchet and start getting along. Life is too short to be negative and hateful."

"Save that speech for her. She's the hater."

"Can we just come to a happy medium?"

"Screw her, my focus is on Gia and Gia only. I mean, for God's sake, she's in ICU fighting for her life and she can't pick up the phone to call you and ask how she's doing? That's messed up."

I couldn't say a word after Jessica laid out the facts of Maria's antics, because she was right. But I couldn't say that to Jessica. Doing that would make me feel like I was talking about Maria behind her back. I wasn't that type of girl.

"The next time you speak with her, you need to tell her that the same shit could happen to her. And I would bet you every dime in my pocket that Gia would check on her to see how she was doing," Jessica added.

"I'm sure she would. But everyone isn't like Gia."

"And you're right. And that's why Gia is special. And as long as she's my friend, I'm gonna have her back and let the whole world know that if someone screws around with her, then they're gonna have to deal with me."

"I'm gonna have her back too," I insisted. "It's the drama of it all, trying to be friends with two girls who don't like each other."

"Then choose a side."

"I'm not gonna do it. I will not allow anyone to tell me what to do, especially when it comes to who I'm gonna allow in my circle."

"But what if you have to choose?"

"Look, I don't wanna have this conversation anymore, Jessica. So let's drop it."

A Bunch of Noisy Bitches

As Jessica and I entered our dorm, we were greeted by a few of the residents. Some I knew and some I didn't. If I didn't know their names, I recognized their faces. I heard some of them whispering amongst themselves and side-eyeing me. It was a telltale sign that they were talking about me, perhaps telling the other girl that I was Gia's roommate.

Jessica moved about saying hi to the ones she knew as we headed toward the elevator. I wasn't in the mood to talk. I wanted to go to my room so I could eat and wind down. After she caught up with me, we stood at the elevator door and waited for it to open. And when it finally did, what do you know, the girl Penny from the top floor was getting off the elevator while we were waiting to get on.

"Hey, you guys, how are you?" she asked. Jessica stood to the side while Penny exited the elevator. I stood alongside Jessica while I spoke back. Jessica said hello, too, but she said it so low that I doubt Penny heard her, and Jessica hopped on the elevator seconds after that.

"Under the circumstances, we're okay," I managed to say

while trying to get on the elevator with Jessica and not being rude by being short with her.

"How is your roommate?" she wanted to know.

Jessica rolled her eyes. "I'll see you upstairs," she told me, and pressed the button for our floor. I watched her as she watched the elevator door close.

"Sorry about your roommate," Penny started off.

"Yeah, we're all sorry. It's crazy, because I just saw her the other day before I left for spring break, and now this," I stated as I moved a few more feet away from the elevator. Didn't want to be in anyone's way as they tried to get on and off. Penny moved in my direction as well.

"So I hear that she's in a coma?"

"Yeah, she is, and that breaks my heart. I hope she gets well and wakes up. I don't know what I would do if I lost her."

"I was here when the paramedics picked her up. Detectives walked around and knocked on everybody's door so they could get some information about her."

"Did they talk to you?"

"Yeah."

"What did they say?" I inquired.

"They pretty much wanted to know if I knew her or the friends that she hung around. They wanted to know if I knew what kind of drugs she used. And if I knew who her dealer was. But I told them that I didn't know much about her. I did tell them that I spoke to you, but that was the extent of it."

"Do you know who else they talked to?" I pressed her for more answers. I needed to know what the cops knew.

"Just a couple of girls in the dorm," she replied. But that wasn't the answer I wanted to hear. I wanted real answers. Answers with some meat on them. I hated being in the dark about something when it pertains to me. I guess everyone does really.

"Any rumors or speculations roaming around here?"

"Yeah, between me and you, a lot of the girls are saying that if she pulls through and comes out of the hospital, the dean isn't going to allow her to come back to school. And this morning I heard my roommate talking to our other roommate, cracking jokes and calling Gia a drug addict. It was horrible to hear. I got up from my bedroom and left the room. Girls can be so insensitive sometimes."

"I'll betcha if they were standing in front of Gia right now, they wouldn't open their freaking mouths," I commented, because I knew what I said was true. There were a lot of phony bitches in the dorm. As a matter of fact, there were a lot of phony bitches on the campus and that's why I dealt with them using a long-handle spoon. And so did Gia. But it's okay, those haters can whatever they want. They wouldn't be able to walk a mile in Gia's shoes. She was a fighter, and she would come out of this. I believed it with all my heart, so I knew it would happen.

"Let me go. I've got things to do," I said, then pressed the button to fetch the elevator. Thank God that it didn't take long, because this Penny girl was wracking my brain. She acted like she could go on and on if I allowed her to.

"All right. Talk to you later."

When I walked into my dorm room, Jessica was sitting on her bed with her hand in a bag of potato chips as she stared at the ceiling. It looked as if she was in deep thought. "What did she have to say?" Jessica asked me.

I sat on the edge of my bed and kicked off my shoes. "She was telling me that a lot of the girls in this building are calling Gia a drug addict. She even said that there's talk about the dean kicking Gia out of school if she pulls through this."

Jessica looked up from her chips. "Fuck the dean! And fuck the bitches that's talking about our friend. The bitches on this campus are so self-righteous. They get on my fucking nerves. I swear, if I hear anyone talking about Gia, I'm gonna get expelled because I am going to kick their ass!" Jessica snapped. I'd never seen her get this angry before, so I could tell that she was really upset about everyone talking about Gia.

"Don't let them get underneath your skin. It's not even worth your time or energy," I told her.

"I know," she said. After pausing a moment, she continued, "It's just that I know she's going through something, so to know that people are calling her names and gossiping about her makes my blood boil."

"Just ignore them."

"I'll try."

"So what's on your mind?" I changed the subject. Continuing to talk about Gia was weighing heavily on my heart. I found myself looking over at her bed a few times, and the thought of her being in the hospital fighting for her life had me on a roller-coaster ride of emotions.

"The guy I met a couple of days ago at Subway. He's trying to see me, but I told him that now wasn't the right time," she started explaining. "He works nearby, at Pizza Hut."

"Why don't you let him come by. Spending time with him could be the distraction you need."

"If I let him stop by, I won't be present. And I can't do that to him. He's a really good guy."

"You'll never know if you don't try it," I encouraged her.

Knock! Knock! Knock! Jessica and I looked at each other. "Who is that?" I whispered.

Jessica shrugged. "I don't know," she whispered back.

Knock! Knock! Knock! Jessica and I were frozen while trying to figure out who was on the other side of the door. Anxiety engulfed me, and I wanted to snap my fingers and disappear. By this time Jessica had stood up, and before she had a chance to take the first step toward the door, the door-knob jiggled as if the person was trying to gain entry. And then the door opened. My mouth opened wide, and so did Jessica's. Her eyes nearly popped out of their sockets too.

My heart dropped to the pit of my stomach as we recognized the person.

"Mr. Santos," Jessica said as she stood there next to her bed. We couldn't believe our eyes. It was Gia's father. And standing behind him was Gia's brother.

The physical contrast between son and father was strong. At five foot eleven, Gia's father was a handsome man with curly black hair. He looked like a sixty-five-year-old retired, out-of-shape wrestler with a beer belly, while his son looked like a seventeen-year-old skateboarder who hung out all day at a skate park.

"You guys didn't hear me knocking?" he asked us.

Jessica sat back down on her bed. "Yeah, we did. But because of what's going on with Gia, we didn't want to be bothered by any of the girls in the dorm," I replied.

"Mind if my son and I come in?"

"Sure, come in," I encouraged him.

After he and Gia's brother walked in the room, they shut the dorm room door. "We came by to collect a few of her things like her purse, state photo ID, social security card, and some other stuff that the hospital admissions office needs," he explained.

Jessica stood back up and grabbed Gia's purse from her closet. "Here it is," she said as she handed it to him. Immediately after Mr. Santos took Gia's purse and other personal belongings, he handed them to Gia's brother.

"This is her bed, right?" he asked as he pointed to the only empty bed in the room.

"Yes, sir," Jessica and I said in unison.

He walked over to it and then sat down on the edge. Gia's brother stepped backward toward the door and leaned against the wall. "You were at the library when she overdosed, right?" he asked Jessica.

Jessica looked petrified, but she willed herself to answer his question. "Yes, sir, I was," she finally responded.

"And you were out of town when it happened?" he turned and asked me.

"Yes, sir." I didn't hesitate to reply.

"Okay, who found her unconscious?" he asked us.

"I'm really not sure, because when I found out and rushed back here, most of the girls that live in this building and the campus security jam-packed the hallway out there while the paramedics worked on Gia in here," Jessica told him. She made sure that she came correct with every word she uttered. Mr. Santos looked intimidating on the surface, but the picture that Gia painted of him when they interact was quite different from the persona he was giving Jessica and me.

"What kind of drugs does she use? And before you say anything, keep in mind that my only daughter is in a coma right now and she needs help. And we can't help her if we don't have the facts. So I beg you to please be straight up with me," he said, and then he fell silent. He looked at me and then looked at Jessica, ready for us to speak.

I looked down at the floor with hopes that Jessica would speak up first.

"Come on, girls, I need the truth and so does my wife. She's back at the hospital bawling her eyes out and praying that God spares Gia's life. She has a lot of life left to live," he pleaded.

I swear, I wanted to break down and tell him everything about what Gia, Jessica, and I did in this room, but I knew that that information would ruin everything for us. Not only would I seal my fate in being kicked out of school, my chances of going to school in another state would be impossibly low. ODU and most other universities have a no tolerance rule about having illegal drugs while on campus. It is a rule that every college enforces.

"Mr. Santos," I started off saying, while trying to think of a plausible answer to give him, "Gia went to see her doctor a few times because she was suffering from depression. Now, I don't know what she was depressed about, because she really didn't talk too much about her personal life, but I do know that her doctor prescribed something to help her with it," I continued.

"No, that's not true. Gia wasn't seeing a doctor. She's on our medical insurance policy, and if she had gone to see a shrink, then her mother and I would've known it," he protested.

The lump that formed in my throat almost made me gag. I thought the excuse I'd made would've been durable, but it blew back in my face. "Maybe she paid the doctor," I added, hoping that this lie was going to work, because at this point I was grasping at straws.

"Stop! That's not what I want to hear. Now tell me the truth, dammit!" he roared. The veins at his temple looked as if they were about to pop.

"Well then, I don't know what else to say." I stuck to my story.

At this moment, his eye color changed. They were bloodshot red. The pupils looked black when he turned his focus toward Jessica. Jessica looked spooked sitting on her bed with her arms crossing each other perfectly on her lap. "Are you gonna lie to me too?" he asked through clenched teeth.

"What do you mean?" Jessica replied, her words barely audible. I noticed immediately that she was about to cave in. Jessica was not stable when put under pressure. She will fold instantly. But right now wasn't the time to do this. I needed the Jessica who was talking shit about the other girls in our dorm, and this Jessica sitting on the bed across from me wasn't that one.

"Tell me what goes on in this room when that door is closed," he instructed as he pointed at the door to our room.

"Nothing really. We have friends come over for study groups. We have girl chats. We watch movies and stuff," she replied.

"How often did Gia take those drugs?" He probed her for more answers.

"Neither one of us know," I interjected, trying to relieve some of the pressure he was giving her.

"I wasn't talking to you," he replied sarcastically as he side-eyed me.

"I know you're not, but you see that you're upsetting her. It's bad enough that she had to see Gia as the paramedics were taking her out of here."

"And you think that me and my wife aren't upset? She's our only little girl. She's the apple of my eye."

"Mr. Santos, if I knew something else, then I would tell you," Jessica finally mustered up the courage to say. I think that if I hadn't spoken up, she wouldn't have opened her mouth to answer him. I guess I pretty much gave her some slack.

"Who is the drug dealer? Give me a name. Number. Something so I can pay him a visit and put him in a bed next to my baby," he pressed us.

"Dad, they don't know," the son blurted out. He sounded like he was tired of being in our room.

Mr. Santos looked at his son and said, "Don't give these girls a pass. Don't you want to know the truth, Ricky?"

"Dad, let's get Gia's stuff and go," his son replied.

Mr. Santos gave Jessica and me a demonic stare, and then he stood up. "God knows what happened, so it will come to light. Mark my words," he commented, and then he and his son left the room without saying good-bye.

Jessica and I looked at each other in disbelief. We didn't say anything for fear that Gia's dad could be standing outside our door. So I jumped up from my bed and tiptoed over to the door. I leaned over and glued my ear to the door to see if I could hear any movement on the other side. The only thing I heard were the other girls who lived in the dorm. Other than that, it was radio silence.

"Think he's out there?" Jessica whispered.

I looked back at her. "Wait," I whispered back, and then I grabbed the doorknob, turned it as quietly as I could, and pulled the door open. No one was standing there, so I opened the door wider and peeped around the corner. I didn't see Mr. Santos or his son anywhere. I looked back at Jessica. "They're gone," I told her.

"Hey, Yoshi, I'm sorry for what happened to your roommate," some random white girl who lives in the building said as she passed by our room.

"Thank you," I replied, and then I closed the door.

"It's time to put our heads together and regroup," I insisted, because it was becoming clear to me and Jessica that everyone was blaming us for what happened to Gia. No one believed that Gia was getting high alone. More important, they didn't believe that we didn't know the drug dealer.

Twenty-Three Hours Later

J essica woke up before I did. She walked into our room holding a laundry basket with clean, folded clothes inside it. She placed the basket on her bed and started putting her things in their rightful place.

"I see you got up and had a head start," I commented as I snuggled underneath my blanket and covered half of my face.

"Yes, I had an overflow in that corner over there and got tired of looking at it." She pointed to a corner on her side of the room.

"Anybody new been asking questions?"

"Nope. It's a ghost town in this dorm. Most of the girls that we saw yesterday left to go home for spring break this morning. I think it's only like six or seven girls left in the entire building."

"Are you going to see Gia today?"

"I've been grappling with that decision all morning. It's like I want to go to show her family that I'm rooting for Gia to get well. But then, when I think about all the eyes that are going to be on me, it makes me want to stay away. I mean, you saw how her dad was acting last night. He wanted to bite our heads off."

"It's funny that you're mentioning this, because I feel the same way. It's like if we go, then we could run into some beef with her family, but if we don't go and check up on her, then we'll look guilty in their eyes like we're hiding something."

"So then what should we do?"

I couldn't answer Jessica's question. We were searching through our hearts and minds and couldn't come up with anything. All we could do was look at each other with blank expressions.

"The frat boys are having a party tomorrow night," Jessica announced.

"Why have a party during spring break when everyone has gone home to visit their family or gone to Cancun?"

"That's the thing. If you have a party with only a few select people going, then there's a slim chance that there would be drama."

"Sounds fun. But I'll pass."

"Why, Yoshi? This little outing could be the thing that'll take our minds off what's going on with Gia. And besides, that frat boy named Conner invited me personally. I've been crushing on him for a while now," Jessica whined, being a brat after crawling onto my bed. I covered my whole face with my blanket. She tugged it, but I held on to it tighter. When she saw that she couldn't pull the blanket away from me, she started tickling me.

"Well then, go."

"Yoshi, I can't go alone. I'll look desperate."

"Well then, don't go."

"When you get invited to a frat party, then you gotta go," she explained. "Please just go with me this one time and I promise that I won't ever ask you again."

I thought for a minute, and then I said, "Okay . . . okay . . . I'll go" between chuckles.

Jessica stopped tickling me. But she continued to hover over me. "You promise?"

"Yes, I promise. But under the condition that I don't have to stay long."

"How long isn't long?" she asked me.

"I'll give you an hour," I told her.

She thought for a second and then replied, "What about an hour and a half?"

"Okay, I can do that. But not a minute longer," I compromised.

"Thank you! Thank you," she responded, and then she leaned over and kissed me on the jaw. I tried to push her back, but she got her kiss in before I could.

"Move," I said with a loud chuckle.

After Jessica kissed me, she hopped off my bed and climbed back on hers. I lay on my bed and looked over at Gia's bed, starting once again to feel bad that she wasn't here. Since I'd been going to ODU, she and I had become so close. She's such a good person with a good heart and I was rooting for her to come out of that situation. I knew that when she'd found out that her boyfriend had cheated on her, she lost it. She took it really bad. I tried to help her along, but it seemed like the only thing that would numb her heart was the pills we used to get high. Before the stresses in life hit her, we would have fun hanging out at sports bars and bowling alleys, doing dinner dates at various restaurants, and getting manicures together. Boy, I missed those times.

Knock! Knock! Knock! Once again, Jessica and I shot a look at each other. "See who it is," she whispered.

"No, you do it," I whispered back.

"Yoshi, Jessica, open the door. It's Lisa."

Jessica got off her bed and opened the door. Lisa was standing there like she had a lot of stuff on her mind.

"Where have you two been?" Lisa asked us as she made her way into the room.

"We've been here. And what's wrong with you?" Jessica answered, closing the door.

"Yeah, what's wrong with you?" I chimed in.

"I just left the hospital, and Gia's parents said that Gia blinked twice and opened her eyes wide once," Lisa replied.

I sat up in my bed, and a burst of happiness engulfed me. It felt great to hear that Gia was getting better. This was the best news that I'd heard for days.

Jessica sat back down on the edge of her bed. "Did you get to see her?" Jessica asked.

Lisa took the chair from under our small desk and sat down. "I didn't see her when she opened her eyes, but I did see her."

"So does that mean that she's out of the coma?" Jessica looked hopeful.

"No, she's still in a coma, but her mother said that when she leaned over the bed and whispered in Gia's ears, that's when Gia's eyes started blinking," Lisa explained.

After Lisa described what happened with Gia, I wanted to beam with excitement, but I knew that from a medical standpoint, a patient in a coma won't move after someone speaks to them. I know this because Sydney had a friend who was put on a ventilator over a decade ago and the guy's family thought that every time they talked to him, he heard their voices and would communicate back to them through movement, but that was far from the truth. However, Gia's brain may still be working to the point that she could hear the sounds around her, like the footsteps of someone approaching or the voice of a person speaking, but again, she was incapable of moving or communicating her awareness.

"Yoshi, did you hear that? Lisa said that Gia moved. She might come out of this," Jessica stated with optimism.

"Yes, I heard her," I replied, trying to be as cheerful as I knew how.

"You guys need to go see her. Who knows, maybe if she hears your voices, she'll wake up," Lisa suggested.

"Yeah, she's right, Yoshi. We ought to go up there."

"You know that as soon as Gia's parents see me, they're gonna start screaming at me. And I don't need that kind of drama right now. Jessica, they like you, so you may wanna go up there on your own."

"Yeah, you might be right," Jessica replied after hearing my reasoning. "Are there a lot of people at the hospital?" Jessica asked Lisa.

"Not really. The only people I saw were her parents, two aunts, and a cousin."

"The grandmother and her brothers weren't there?"

"Nope."

"Were Gia's aunts and cousins nice to you?" Jessica probed.

"If saying hi was nice, then I guess so."

"Are you going back to the hospital to see her today? Because I'll go if you go with me," Jessica said.

"Yes, if you want me to. But it's gonna have to be after I get my hair done."

"What time is your appointment?" Jessica wanted to know.

"In two hours," Lisa said.

"When do you think that you'll be done?"

"All I'm getting is a doobie, so maybe an hour and a half."

"All right, then meet me back here when you're done and then we'll leave," Jessica asked.

I sat there and watched as Jessica made plans with Lisa to go to the hospital to pay Gia a visit. I felt sad because I took one trip to the hospital and was treated like a villain and had no choice but to leave. It made me feel so messed up knowing that Gia's family didn't want me there. I loved Gia like she was my blood relative. We did almost everything together. I've laughed with her, cried with her, and counseled her when she needed advice. So not seeing her has been breaking my heart into a thousand pieces.

"Are you all right?" Lisa asked me.

Jessica turned her attention toward me. "Yes, what's wrong?" she chimed in.

Before I could reply to either of them, Jessica got up from her bed, crawled onto mine, and embraced me. The warmth from her touch engulfed me, and I couldn't hold back the tears.

"Yoshi, why are you crying?" Jessica asked, and I cried several more tears. She used the back of her hands to help dry my eyes and cheeks.

Lisa got up from her chair and came to sit down beside me. She also embraced me. "Why are you crying?" she said.

"Because Gia's parents won't let me see Gia. They think that I'm the reason she's in the hospital," I sobbed as my tears forced open the floodgates.

Jessica started rubbing my back in a circular motion. "Yoshi, that's not true," Jessica said, trying to make me feel differently.

"Yes, that's not true," Lisa agreed.

"I know y'all are trying to make me feel better. But I know the truth. Both of Gia's parents screamed at me yesterday, so they're gonna make sure that I don't get to see Gia," I explained as my sobbing continued.

"I'll tell you what," Jessica started off. "When Lisa and I go back to see Gia, we'll try to use the telephone in her room and call you and tell you how she's doing while we're in the room with her—that is, if none of her family are in there."

"You will?" I replied, feeling a little hopeful.

"Yep, I'm gonna do just that," Jessica insisted. "I don't know why I didn't think of that at first."

Feeling overjoyed with excitement, I thanked Lisa and Jessica. This made my day.

A Day I'll Never Forget

I finally got that call from Jessica and Lisa, but they weren't using the telephone in Gia's room. They told me that they were using one of the pay phones on the first floor. I was bummed out, but hey, what can I say? I can't control everything in this world, even though I wished I did. During our conversation they mentioned that Gia's condition was still the same but everyone was being optimistic that things would change for the better. I felt the same way.

Hours passed by after we hung up, and all I did with my time was stay in my room and blame myself for leaving Gia here in this room all alone. While I sulked in a bucket of tears, Jessica walked back into our room and reminded me about the party I'd promised I would attend.

"Come on, Yoshi, you promised me that you'd go. So get out of that bed right now," she badgered me.

"Please, not tonight. I promise I will do something else with you. Like, I'll take you to lunch tomorrow and buy you whatever you want." I tried negotiating with her.

"Nope, that's not gonna work. So come on," she pressured me as she dragged me out of the bed. "Come on, Yoshi, it's gonna be fun. And it'll help take your mind off everything that's going on. And you know this is what Gia would want you to do."

I inhaled and then exhaled after I stood up. "Okay, I'll go, but I am not changing clothes," I stated.

"That's fine. I'll take you as you are."

Jessica grabbed me and we left our room. When we walked outside, I couldn't believe how dark it had gotten. It was a little after eight o'clock.

"I'm not staying long," I told her.

"Stay at least one hour and then you can leave," she compromised as we walked arm-in-arm toward the frat house only a block away.

As we walked up the walkway of the frat house, Jessica zoomed in on Conner standing next to two other girls with a beer in his hand. "Look at those tricks standing next to my future boyfriend," she yelled over the loud music.

I chuckled because Jessica was not feeling those girls smiling all in Conner's face. "Go over there and say something. Let him know that you're here," I encouraged. But before she could do it, he spotted us and immediately excused himself from the girls and walked over to where we were standing.

"How you ladies doing?" Conner asked us, and then he took a gulp of beer from his bottle.

Jessica turned her frown into a smile. "We're doing good."

"I'm glad that you accepted my invitation." He spoke directly to Jessica.

"I wasn't going to miss it for the world," she replied. "And I thought I was gonna have to pull you away from the girls over there when I first walked in."

"Oh, they're nobodies. Just a couple of girls from around campus."

"Did you invite them too?" Jessica wouldn't let up.

"No, I didn't invite them. One of my other frat brothers did. It's my job to show everyone southern hospitality," he said. But the phrase *full of shit* was written all over him. He had Jessica grinning from ear to ear, but I wasn't charmed at all.

"Want something to drink? We've got vodka, tequila, and beer," Conner offered.

"I'll take a beer," I said.

"I'll take some tequila," she replied all giddy.

"Be right back," he said.

As soon as he walked away, I turned my attention to Jessica. "Don't get wasted on me."

"Don't worry, I won't. And anyway, stop being a party pooper! And let's enjoy ourselves. Do it for Gia, because if she wasn't in the hospital, she would be here too," Jessica added.

I saw that there was no way that I was going to get through to Jessica, so I took a deep breath, exhaled, and began to vibe to the music.

From the looks of the attendees, the guys and girls seemed to be having a good time. I counted eight girls and fifteen or sixteen guys. The deejay was playing music from Biz Markie, Dr. Dre and Snoop Dogg, and LL Cool J. I had to admit that this scenery was changing my mood a bit.

Jessica started rocking back and forth and swaying her hips from side to side as she grooved to Outkast's new song. I stood there alongside her, and in seconds I joined in and started grooving to the beat of the music. Jessica looked at me like she couldn't believe that I was bobbing my head to the beat, and then she smiled.

"See, I knew this would be a good idea," she yelled over the loud music.

I shrugged my shoulders and continued to dance. Three minutes into the groove of things, Conner came back with the beer for me, and he handed Jessica a cup of tequila. He also came back with one of the head frat guys named Tyler. "I'm surprised to see you here." He leaned in toward me, yelling over the music while Conner entertained Jessica only a few feet away from me.

"I am too," I replied.

Tyler was one of the white boys who flirted with me a few days ago while he was walking by my dorm with his cronies. On that day, I felt like he was being disrespectful when he asked me to come see him so he could fuck me. His other frat brother, Conner, tried to flirt with me too. Now he was standing a few feet away, talking to Jessica. Both of them were being assholes that day. But for some reason, both of them were acting like gentlemen now.

"We're going over here to sit down," Jessica said, yelling loud enough so that I could hear her.

"I know how much you like that guy, so don't get missing," I yelled back.

She smiled and winked. "I'll try," she commented, and she left me standing there to talk to Tyler.

"Can I ask you a question?" I started off after I turned back around to face him.

"Yes, of course."

"Why were you and your frat brothers being so disrespectful to me the other day?" I yelled over the music.

He smiled and said, "First off, let me say sorry. Do you accept my apology?" he yelled back.

I paused for a second and then I said, "Yes, but don't do that again."

"I won't. Trust me, I won't."

"Now tell me why you did it?"

"Look at you, you're beautiful. You intimidated me."

"How did I intimidate you when I didn't utter one word to you?"

"That's the thing. When I started flirting with you, you didn't respond. I'm used to girls giving me attention and falling down at my feet. But you wouldn't do it. So that's why me and my frat brothers started heckling you. But now that I have the privilege to be in your company, I have a chance to make things right and show you that I'm really not that kind of guy."

Tyler was very handsome. Another Luke Perry, if you ask me. Tyler was a few inches taller and he had a stronger build, that of an athlete. He had rhythm too. And he seemed to love dancing to Biz Markie.

"You like this song?" I asked him after taking a sip from the bottle of beer.

"Yeah, I love this guy. He's a really good rapper," he replied while he bobbed his head.

"How long have you been listening to rap music?" I asked.

"For a while now. My parents don't like it, but hey, what can you say to an adult?" he yelled.

"I guess you got a point."

"So, where is your boyfriend?"

"I don't have one. I think being single has its advantages. Being stress-free is one of them," I mentioned. "What about you? I heard the girls on campus love you. You're like the king around here," I commented after taking another sip of beer.

"Follow me over here so we can talk more," he instructed, and led us to a cloth fabric futon in the corner of their entertainment room.

"So, why are you here during spring break?" he asked immediately after we sat down next to each other.

"I went home for two days and then I decided to come back," I told him. "And why are you still on campus?"

"My parents are at their vacation house in the Hamptons, and I wasn't feeling that scene so I elected to stay on campus."

"Hey, wait, you're from New York?"

"Yep, born and raised."

"I'm from New York too. My mom and stepfather live in Manhattan."

"Small world. I mean, who would've thought?" he said, and smiled. "Do you like football?"

"No, not really. I mean, I don't watch it because I don't understand it."

"So you've never seen me play?"

"I did when I went to the homecoming game. But that's it."

"Did you have fun?"

"I only went because I wanted to see the band perform. I love our band."

"That's it?" he asked, giving me a cheesy smile. He looked a little embarrassed.

"Yep, that's it," I assured him. I mean, why lie? I'm not boosting this guy's ego. He's got enough guys and girls doing it.

"You're roommates with that girl Gia, right?"

"Yes, why?"

"How is she doing? I heard she was in ICU."

"Yeah, she's lying in a coma, but we're confident that she'll come out of it," I lied. I wanted to tell him how I really felt, but I didn't want to speak negatively about her situation and then cause something bad to happen.

"Is it true that she overdosed?" His questions continued.

"Yes. But I wasn't there. I was in New York, so then I hopped back on a flight so I could be by her side."

"That's really nice of you."

"I'm just doing what she'd do if I was in that situation."

"I'm sure she would," he agreed. "So what do you like to do for fun?" He changed the subject. I was glad that he did, because it didn't feel good to talk about Gia. I came here to get my mind off her situation, not be reminded of it.

"I like going to the movies. I like shopping, bike riding,

doing at least one spa day a week. Oh yeah, and I love to bowl too," I commented, then finished the rest of the beer in my bottle.

"No way. Really?! I love bowling too," he replied with excitement. "We've gotta get together and go sometime. You can come with your roommate and I can bring my frat brother. I mean, will you look at them over here," he said, and pointed at those two laughing and drinking. It looked like she was having the time of her life.

"Sure, let's do that." I accepted his offer. The whole idea seemed like it would be fun. The longer I sat with Tyler, the more I liked him. He wasn't the brash, self-centered prick I once pegged him to be. This new person was funny, charming, attentive, and interesting.

He and I sat there and talked for hours, it seemed like. He fed me pizza and grabbed me a couple more beers from the cooler, which had me intoxicated to the tenth power. Between the music, Tyler's funny jokes, and the alcohol, I was on cloud nine. This whole night out definitely did me some good, and I had Jessica to thank for it.

As Tyler and I continued to entertain each other, Jessica appeared.

"Ready?" she asked. She looked like she was more intoxicated than I was.

"You mean go back to the dorm?" I yelled over the loud and intense music.

"Yes, I'm tired. Plus, I have a hair appointment in the morning and I need some sleep."

I turned and looked at Tyler. "I guess my gig is up," I commented, then smiled.

"But I don't want you to leave," he protested in a kind and sexy manner.

"She and I came here together. And besides, I can't let her walk to the dorm alone. It's after midnight."

"Be right back," he said.

I watched him as he got up from the futon and walked to the other side of the room. He leaned over in the direction of Conner's ear and said something to him. Two seconds later, Tyler and Conner headed in our direction.

"He's gonna be a gentleman and walk you back to your dorm so I can spend a little bit more time with this beautiful young lady here," he announced, looking at Jessica and then looking at me. I had to admit that this guy was jumping all the hoops to show me that he's a stand-up kind of guy.

Jessica looked at me and then she looked at Conner. "Okay, well, if he doesn't mind," she finally replied.

"Of course he doesn't," Tyler said.

"Yeah, I'm down. Come on," he told Jessica, and then they turned to leave.

"Don't stay out too late," Jessica yelled over the music after looking back over her shoulder.

"I won't," I yelled back.

Tyler and I watched as his frat brother escorted Jessica out of the house. "Now I got you all to myself," he said, leaning in.

I side-eyed him and gave him a half smile.

"Don't be looking at me like that. I like you, and I can tell that you like me too," he said confidently.

"You think so, huh?" I got a little cocky.

"I know so," he insisted, and then he moved in closer. Before I knew it, his lips were on mine and sparks started flying. We moved our lips with the right precision, and the moistness of our tongues felt like magic. We did this for at least thirty seconds if not more. Butterflies filled my tummy while my heart exploded into little pieces. This guy was really a good kisser.

"Follow me," he instructed, and grabbed me by the hand after he stood up.

I willingly stood and followed him. He led me upstairs to a

bedroom on the second floor. There were two full-size beds in the room.

"Whose room is this?" I wanted to know.

"It's me and my roommate's room. Why?"

"No reason really," I told him.

"Are you sure?" he pressed me.

"Yes, I'm sure," I assured him. But for some reason, I was having doubts.

"Okay, good," he said as he pulled me toward a bed that I figured was his. I followed him as he backed up. It took us a total of six steps to get to the bed. After he sat down on the edge of it, he guided me into his arms. The feelings from his touch were unexplainable. It just felt right.

Tyler wasted no time feeling me and kissing me on my stomach. When he slid his hands up my shirt and started massaging my breasts and rubbing my nipples, it sent me out into space. I started moaning and biting my bottom lip from the sheer joy and passion of this escapade.

"Come to me," he said as he pulled me on top of him and lay back on the bed. But I wasn't on top of him for long, because he turned me over onto my back and started gyrating his dick against my pussy. We were both still clothed, but the spark was there.

Between the kissing and touching, I felt Tyler's dick get harder with each grind. As the kissing and gyrating became more intense, I watched him as he climbed off me and stood up from the bed.

"I'm gonna fuck the shit out of you," he said as he unzipped his pants and pulled them off.

"Oh no, dude, I didn't come upstairs for this. And I don't even know you like that," I told him, and sat up on his bed.

"I'm not trying to hear that shit. Lay your ass back down!" he roared. His face looked menacing as he pushed me back on the bed, yanked my pants off, and then climbed back on me.

"Get off me!" I demanded while pushing him, but he was too strong.

"You better shut the fuck up, you whore, before I make you wish that you never laid eyes on me."

"Tyler, what are you doing? Trying to rape me?"

"I'm not raping you. You begged for this dick all night long and now I'm gonna give it to you," he stated, all while gritting his teeth.

"Get off me," I screamed, hoping that one of his buddies in the house would hear me and come to my rescue. But no one came, so I screamed again. "Move, Tyler, get off me!" I yelled while trying to push him. My screams went unheard, but I wasn't going to give up. I knew that if I continued to fight him, then he'd get the message that I didn't want to have sex with him.

While he was using most of his strength to pin both of my arms down, I figured that if I used my knee to plunge him in his groin area, the pain alone would paralyze him long enough so that I could get off the bed, out of this room, and out of this house without any blowback.

By this time, he had secured my arms, but when he realized that he needed to use one of his hands to guide his penis inside me, he elected to gyrate and steer his body and hoped it would let him achieve his goal, but it didn't. So he released my arm and reached down between my legs to grab his dick. As soon as he did that, I kneed him in his stomach, missing his groin area by a couple of inches, and this infuriated him.

"Fucking bitch! You just tried to knee me in my cock?" he roared. His facial expression was menacing. And before I could utter one word, he backhanded me with two loud and painful slaps. *Whack! Whack!* I swear to God, I saw stars in that dark-ass room. But that wasn't enough. Through clenched teeth he said, "Do that again and I will fucking kill you, you dumb bitch!"

I believed every word Tyler uttered. The impact of his

blows on me was a sign that he had the capability to kill me if he wanted to.

I lay there and watched him as he pulled his penis through the open part of his boxer briefs and then shoved it inside of me. The first touch by the head of his penis hit me like a ton of bricks. But I take it that he enjoyed it, because after he initially pushed himself inside of me, he pulled out and then inserted himself once again. Before I knew it, he started penetrating me. I couldn't watch him, though. I turned my head and faced the wall nearest me. I tried to think of a lot of things that I could be doing rather than being in this situation. I try to think of what I would do tomorrow versus what I was doing right then. While I forced myself to take my mind out of this wretched and sordid scene, I heard the sound of someone trying to open the bedroom door. Too bad for me, because they couldn't get in. Tyler had already locked the door.

"Aye, yo dude, you're in there?" I heard a guy's voice yell from the other side.

"Yeah, give me a minute," Tyler replied.

I had to keep lying there while this rapist held me hostage and took away my rights and my freedom to do what I wanted with my body. He was a monster. He was inhuman. And why me? Despite what he said, I never gave him the impression that I wanted to have sex with him tonight. I only came here to socialize, get a few drinks, listen to some music. It was bad enough that my roommate was fighting for her life. I was in this terrible situation. Believe it or not, she and I were both fighting for our lives, period. All I could ask was, Why me? I'd never done anything horrible or hurt anyone. What was happening to me was barbaric. I wished I could snap my fingers and be gone at that very moment. Is this how women feel when they're being raped? Is this how we are supposed to treat a woman or someone weaker than you? It seemed as if the more times he penetrated me, the louder his moans and sounds of ecstasy got.

I was beginning to feel sick to my stomach. I felt like I wanted to get out of my own skin. My thoughts began to spin around my head, trying to figure out how much longer I was going to be in this situation. I said a quiet prayer to God and told him that if he would get me out of there, I would change my ways. That I would never put myself in another setting like this. A minute after I ended my prayer, Tyler ejaculated inside of me and then collapsed on top of me. A few seconds later, he rolled off me and onto his back.

"You really got some good pussy," he said through his heavy breaths.

I didn't utter one word. Instead, I got off the bed, grabbed my pants, and stormed out of the bedroom. I didn't look back as I raced down the flight of stairs. There were only a handful of people in their entertainment room that I had to walk by to get out of the house. They all looked up at me and watched me go.

At that point, I could not have cared less about putting on my clothes. I just wanted to get away from Tyler as far and fast as I could. My heart was hurting. I was filled with anxiety and betrayal, and my adrenaline was flowing rapidly. I was also embarrassed that I had to leave that house with everyone looking at me. This was a moment that I'd never forget.

As soon as I stepped out in the frigid air, the reality that I needed to put my pants on hit me hard. Not anywhere near the frat house, though. So as soon as I had gotten about 400 feet away from the four walls of male testosterone, I found a tree and used it as leverage to slide on my pants. After I was clothed from the waist down, I continued on to my dorm.

The walk to my dorm was only about fifty yards, but it

seemed like it was taking me forever to get there. I don't know if it was the fact that the walk was actually longer or that my mind was playing tricks on me. Either way, it was taking a toll on me, so I ran the rest of the way.

When I finally made it to my dorm, I saw a figure of a woman staring down at me. I squinted and tried to refocus my eyes to get a better sense of who it was, but by the time I blinked, she was gone. So, without further delay, I used my electronic key to gain access to the building, and after the door opened, I jumped on the elevator and headed to my room.

Immediately after I stepped in my room, I noticed that Jessica was in her bed and sound asleep. I wanted so badly to wake her and tell her what had just happened to me, but I decided against it for fear that she wouldn't believe me. But I did get into the shower. The smell of Tyler and his body fluids that were on and inside of me made me feel yucky, and dirty. So, after I disrobed, I headed into the shower with the ambition to come out clean.

Crying Wolf

The one-hour session in the shower didn't do anything for my mental state. I was clean physically, but emotionally I was damaged and starting to feel physically shut down. So I climbed into my bed and tried to make myself go to sleep, but it didn't work. I tossed and turned all night. I even got out of my bed and paced the floor of my dorm room. But even then I couldn't trigger my body to become calm.

I did, however, crawl back in my bed and force my eyes to close. Hours had gone by, and the reason I knew this was because I got a couple of nudges from Jessica with attempts to wake me up. I opened my eyes and saw sunlight. While I was glad that I had fallen asleep, the knowledge and pain that happened to me the night before were still standing right there in my face.

Jessica was all smiles and cheers. She sat there on her bed and started pressuring for details of how my night ended with Tyler.

"What time did you come back this morning?" she started off saying.

I lay there on my bed with my blanket pulled up to my neck while I stared up at the ceiling. I took a deep breath and then exhaled. I opened my mouth to say something, but I couldn't utter a word. And at that very moment, my eyes started filling up with tears, and then my throat felt as if it had a piece of hair caught up in the back. I swear, I couldn't get it together, mentally or physically.

"Come on now, give me the details," she pressed as she rubbed her hands together.

"Jessica, he raped me." I finally got up the gumption to say it, and then I turned on my side and faced her. From there, she saw the tears falling from my eyes.

Without hesitation, she got off her bed and joined me on mine. She sat down next to me. "What do you mean, he raped you?"

"After you left, he and I went upstairs to a room that he shares with another guy, and no one was in there but me and him. So we started kissing. But after doing that for a few minutes, he stood up from the bed and started taking his pants off. When I saw him doing that, I was like, hey what are you doing? And he said that he was going to give me what I had been wanting all night. So I'm like, what are you talking about? I don't wanna have sex with you, and then I sat up and tried to get off the bed. But he pushed me back on the bed and told me that I wasn't going anywhere. He hit me in my face twice when I kneed him in his stomach. He even threatened to kill me if I tried to get up or move again," I explained, and then I broke down in tears.

"Oh my God! I can't believe he did this to you," Jessica replied, and embraced me as tightly as she could. To feel the comforting warmth of her body made me feel like I wasn't alone.

"Jessica, do you know how it feels to be raped? This guy took my body and did whatever he wanted to do with it, and

I couldn't stop him. Do you know how that shit feels?" I continued to sob between words.

Jessica loosened her embrace and separated us. She leaned me back just enough for us to look each other in the face. "Have you told anyone else this?" she wanted to know.

"No."

Jessica let out a long sigh. "That's good, because we're gonna have to figure some things out first."

"Like what?" I wondered aloud.

"Are you planning to press rape charges against Tyler?"

"Yes."

"When do you plan to do it?"

"I don't know."

"What do you mean that you don't know? This is a serious matter." Jessica started scolding me. "Did you take a shower when you got back to the dorm?"

"Yeah."

"Why did you do that, Yoshi? All the evidence was inside of you. You were supposed to go to the hospital and have a rape test done on you."

"I didn't think about it. I just felt so dirty that I wanted to wipe his smell off me."

Jessica let out another long sigh, and then she stood up from my bed. "Did anyone see him raping you?" Jessica's questions continued as she started pacing the bedroom floor. She walked to the door and then turned around and walked to the window.

"No, we were in the room by ourselves. But when I finally got out of there, I ran downstairs and everyone left in the house saw me with my pants in my hands."

"That's not good enough."

"What'cha mean that's not good enough?"

"Everyone you saw in that house will act like they never saw you, so it would be your word versus his."

"So what do you think I should do?"

"I don't know, Yoshi. This one is gonna be hard."

"Why do you say that?"

"Because no one in that house is going to have your back. Tyler is the best football player that our school has. He is loved by all the hoes on this campus. The tramps on campus would've loved to be in your place last night. I saw a handful of girls watching as you and Tyler hugged up and kissed in the corner all night. You should've seen their stank-ass faces. So do you think someone is going to take your word over his?" Jessica stated.

"You're acting like I'm gonna report him to the campus police. I'm gonna go downtown to the Norfolk Police Department."

"And you think that that's gonna make a difference? Yoshi, you should've gone to the hospital last night and had a rape test done on you. Without that, I don't think that you have a case."

I sat there and listened to Jessica's every word. But something inside me spoke louder. I was raped. And Tyler knew he raped me too. So that's all I needed to take to the cops and let them decide.

Knock! Knock! Knock! Jessica looked at the door from where she was standing in the middle of the floor. "Who is it?" Jessica asked.

"It's me, Penny, from upstairs."

Jessica looked at me and then looked back at the door. "Who are you looking for?" Jessica asked her.

"Is Yoshi in there?" she replied.

Jessica looked back at me. "What'cha want me to say?" she whispered.

"I don't know," I whispered back, because in reality, right now wasn't a good time to entertain anyone with all that I had on my plate.

"Think she heard us talking?" Jessica's questions continued.

"I don't know," I answered, and then our dorm room telephone rang.

"Hello," Jessica said after she grabbed the phone from the desk.

While Jessica had gotten caught in a conversation with the caller, Penny stood on the other side of our door. I couldn't in good conscience leave her standing out there, so I climbed out of my bed and opened the door.

"Hey, what's up?" I forced myself to say. Mind you, I was going through something mind-blowing and I wasn't in the mood to have a visitor.

"I was just coming to check on you," she said, looking at me from head-to-head.

"I'm fine," I replied, giving a puzzled look and wondering if she'd heard Jessica and me talking a few minutes ago.

"You sure?"

"Of course I'm sure," I said, becoming a bit annoyed.

"Well, it's just that I saw you from my window late last night, running to our dorm by yourself. I raced out of my room to make sure that you were all right, but by the time I got to the main lobby, you had already gotten on the elevator," she explained.

"No, don't say that. That's not true," I heard Jessica say behind me. Penny and I both turned our focus on Jessica. A few seconds later, she collapsed on the floor. The cordless telephone handset fell out of her hand and slid across the floor. Penny and I sprinted into action.

"Jessica, are you all right?" I spoke loudly in her ear. I even tapped her on her face a few times. "Jessica, wake up," I continued as I tapped her again.

Slowly she started coming out of it. She started blinking, and then her mouth started moving. "That's right. Wake up.

I'm here for you," I assured her as I brushed her hair back with the palm of my hand.

"Is it true?" she finally said, after looking at me and then at Penny.

"Is what true?" I wanted to know.

"Where is the phone?" she asked.

"It's right here," Penny said as she grabbed the phone, which was only a few feet away.

Penny handed me the cordless telephone, and I handed it to Jessica. "Who were you talking to on the phone?" I questioned her.

"It was Lisa. She said Gia was dead. She died in the coma," Jessica finally explained. Her words hit me like a ton of bricks.

"No way. That can't be true. We gotta call her parents," I protested.

Jessica sat up on her butt. I got up from the floor, grabbed my sweatpants from my closet, and slipped them on. I also grabbed a pair of socks and my sneakers while I was in there.

"Where are you going?" Jessica asked me.

"I'm going to the hospital to see it for myself," I told her.

"But you're not driving."

"I'm taking a cab."

"Wait for me, I'll drive," Jessica insisted.

"Come on," I said. By this time I was grabbing my purse from the desk near my bed.

"I am so sorry to hear about your roommate," Penny stated.

"We appreciate it. Thank you," I replied as I made my way to the door of our room. Penny followed me.

"If you need anything, just let me know," she announced.

"Thank you," Jessica said as she grabbed her car keys and her purse.

I walked out of the room first. Penny followed me, and Jessica followed her. After Jessica locked the door to our room, she and I took the elevator down. As soon as the elevator door opened on the first floor and we stepped off, the roomful of women who lived in our dorm had eyes on us. I hated being the center of attention, so I moved quickly toward the exit.

The ride to the hospital was quiet. Neither Jessica nor I said one word to each other. But it was quite apparent that we were mulling over different scenarios concerning Gia. The thought of her dying just seemed unimaginable. We had so much stuff that we planned to do. Places to go and food to eat. So there's got to be a mistake. Jessica had to have heard Lisa's words wrong. Nevertheless, things would be revealed when we saw them ourselves.

Finally, we made it to the hospital, and as soon as Jessica parked her car, we made a dash into the building. There was an elevator near the entrance of the visitors' lobby, so we took it to the Intensive Care Unit. Waiting for the elevator to arrive, I was feeling a panic attack coming on. To have that with the feeling that I might pass out at any given second was almost too much to bear.

Ding . . . I looked up and realized that the elevator door had opened. Jessica stepped off first, and I followed her. From where we were on the ICU floor, Jessica and I could hear voices coming from the direction we were walking toward. A faint sound was like crying.

"Do you hear that?" I asked Jessica.

"Yeah, I hear it," she replied as we continued to walk that way.

"Think Gia's parents will let me see her?" I asked. I needed to hear Jessica say that Gia's parents would be okay that I was there to mourn Gia along with them.

"What kind of question is that? Of course they will. She's gone now. And nothing can bring her back," Jessica told me.

I took a deep breath and then exhaled as we moved on.

I allowed Jessica to walk ahead of me so I could hide behind her. I wanted to gauge the atmosphere before I stepped in it. I wanted to see who were all there and feel out their temperament. So the moment Jessica and I turned the corner and walked down the hallway of Gia's room, I zoomed in and saw who was there. I saw Lisa and Chelsea first. I also saw Gia's brother Ricky and father. But I didn't see Gia's mother or her grandmother. There were two other people there that I didn't recognize. I was sure that those two girls could be related to Gia, especially with all the crying they were doing.

As Jessica and I walked up, Lisa and Chelsea walked up to us and embraced us. I made sure that there was a little distance between me and Gia's family. As a matter of fact, I pulled them a few feet away and turned my back on them just in case Gia's mother walked up and saw me.

"What's going on?" I started off.

"Yeah, is Gia in her room?" Jessica chimed in.

"Yes, she's in the room. The doctor took her off the ventilator and she died almost an hour ago," Lisa answered.

"How does she look?" I wanted to know, since I hadn't seen her in the hospital.

"She still looks like she's asleep," Chelsea said.

"Who's in the room? I wanna see her," I stated.

"Her mother and her grandmother are. They've been in there since Gia was taken off life support."

"Damn!" I blurted softly.

"What's wrong?" Lisa asked me.

"Her mother isn't gonna let me go in that room and see Gia," I expressed. "They already got it in their heads that it was my fault that Gia was taking drugs."

"I don't think so. Her mother and grandmother were just

in there praying a few minutes ago. So I don't think that they'll say anything mean to you," Chelsea insisted.

"Yeah, Yoshi, I don't think they'll say anything to you," Lisa agreed.

I listened to Lisa and Chelsea as they encouraged me to go see Gia. They had more pros than cons, so eventually I sided with them and took a leap of faith. "You guys have to go in there with me," I bargained.

"Sure, come on," Lisa insisted, and grabbed my hand.

I pulled back from her.

"What's wrong?" she asked me.

"I'll feel better walking behind you guys," I said.

"Well, just walk behind me," Jessica replied, and then we all turned toward Gia's hospital room and started walking.

Before I could walk three steps, all of us were stopped in our tracks.

"Where the hell do you think that you're going?!" Gia's father roared. The thunder in his voice bounced off the walls in the hallway. Lisa, Jessica, and Chelsea gave him a look of fear. But there was no fear in my eyes or heart. I only felt disappointment. I also felt singled out.

"I called and told her of Gia's passing, and I told them to come up here and pay their respects." Lisa spoke first.

"How could you call the person responsible for my daughter's death to come here?" he asked Lisa as he stormed toward us.

"Mr. Santos, I didn't kill Gia. I was in New York visiting my family." I tried to reason with him.

"Who's out there?" I heard Gia's mother's voice coming from the left side of the hallway.

"This tyrant is here to see our daughter," Mr. Santos pointed out.

"You got some nerve coming up here to see my daughter. Don't you think that you've done enough to her?"

At that very moment, I stood there before Gia's parents

and felt like an outcast. I felt bullied and I felt alone. Everyone around me was silent, except for Gia's parents. And it seemed like the louder they talked, the more I felt defeated. So I had to do something. Something that would let everyone on that floor know that I was tired of being the culprit.

"Mr. and Mrs. Santos," I started off saying, "I didn't kill Gia. I was in New York with my family. I loved Gia. She was like a sister to me. So why take me through all of this? I didn't shove those drugs down her throat. If I did anything to her, it was to love her. You have no idea how many nights I let her cry in my arms when stuff didn't go her way. She was heartbroken about a lot of things. Some things I knew, and some things I didn't. And guess what? I didn't force it out of her. When she wanted some alone time, Jessica and I would give it to her by leaving our room. So don't keep blaming me for her death. It's killing me inside right now that I won't be able to see or spend time with her anymore." I stood there waiting for their rebuttal.

"Somebody get this bitch away from me before I choke her ass!" Mrs. Santos demanded as her eyes got larger.

Lisa felt the anger and hurt in Gia's mother's heart, and that's when she grabbed me by the arm and led me in the opposite direction. "Come on," she said.

"Yes, get her the fuck outta here," I heard Gia's father shout behind me. "I'm coming to get my daughter's things by tomorrow, so don't be there when I show up." He continued to shout demands at me. I ignored him and kept walking.

"Did you see that shit?" I asked Lisa as she escorted me to the elevator.

She pressed the elevator button as she stood next to me. "Of course I did. I was right there," she replied hesitantly.

"Why are they treating me like that?" My questions continued as tears started falling from my eyes. I wiped some of them away with my fingertips.

"Because they don't know what kind of person you are. They don't see the loving and kind person that Gia saw in you. Their eyes won't let them. They need someone to blame, and unfortunately that someone is you," Lisa pointed out, and then the elevator door opened. She got on it, and I followed. We both stood there and waited for the door to close, but a hand blocked the doors from closing. When the doors rolled back, I was shocked to see Gia's brother standing there. He looked like he'd been crying all day.

"I just wanna say how sorry I am about how my parents are treating you. Gia and I talked a lot these past couple of months, and she said nothing but good things about you. I know for a fact that she loved you like a sister. She said that you guys were best friends."

"I appreciate you coming here and telling me that," I told him.

"Don't mention it. I mean, that was the least I could do. Now take care of yourself," he replied as the elevator doors moved to close.

"You do the same," I said as they shut.

Lisa and I looked at each other.

"Did you just hear that?" I asked cheerfully. It felt like a heavy burden was lifted from my shoulders.

She smiled and embraced me. "Yes, I did. Now, tell me how you feel knowing what he just said?"

"I feel good under the circumstances. To know that Gia loved me and to make mention of it to her brother was all I needed. It's unfortunate that her parents don't know. But hey, you can't have it all."

Don't Fuck with Me!

By the time the elevator door opened, Lisa had agreed to take me back to campus since Jessica was staying at the hospital and I didn't have a ride. The ride was only about ten minutes, but in that time we had a lot to say.

"Will you be all right going back to the dorm?" Lisa wanted to know.

"Yeah, I'm sure I will," I replied, gazing out at the sky. There were at least a dozen blackbirds flying around, circling one another. They looked like they didn't have a care in the world. They looked free and adventurous. What would I pay to be one of them now?

"Got something to eat back in your room?" Her questions continued.

"Trust me, food is the last thing on my mind right now," I assured her.

"Well, call me if you need anything," she insisted as she pulled alongside the street on the east side of campus.

"I will. Thanks," I replied, and exited her car.

My dorm was only a quarter of a mile from where Lisa

dropped me off, so the walk wouldn't take long. It was a Sunday afternoon, and only a handful of people were walking around. Spring break would be over in three days, so the influx of students would be rejoining us soon. I wasn't looking forward to it, though. It was much quieter with fewer students roaming around campus, and I loved it that way.

"Hey, Yoshi, why did you leave so soon? We were in the middle of getting to know each other," I heard a male voice say, and I knew instantly who was behind that voice. I tried to ignore him by not turning my attention toward him. I even picked up speed to get to my dorm.

"Come on, Yoshi, you don't have to act like that," Tyler shouted.

"Yeah, Yoshi, don't act like that. We're all friends here," Conner shouted. "I heard that you're quite the kisser."

"Yeah, me too," another guy chimed in. I had no idea what his name was, but I knew he was one of Tyler's frat brothers. "Can I have you the next time you come over?" he continued.

By now, it was three guys annoying me by trying to create a scene with a dozen students who were walking by us. I couldn't take it any longer and hurled obscenities at them.

"Fuck you! And how dare you act like I wanted to fuck you last night. You fucking raped me, you monster!" I spewed at him while gritting my teeth.

Hearing the word *rape* seemed to hit Tyler with a mighty blow. I swear, I'd never seen a man run so fast. As soon as I uttered the word, he raced toward me, grabbed my neck, and lifted me up from the ground. "Bitch, if you ever say that I raped you again, I will personally kill you. Do you understand?"

I was gagging and coughing, trying to pry his hands off me. But his strength was much greater than mine.

"You let her go right now," I heard someone say in the distance.

Tyler released his grip from my neck, and I collapsed on the ground. "So what are you, her bodyguard?" Tyler questioned a white guy who was walking a few feet away from us.

"Why don't you pick on someone your own size?" the guy lectured Tyler as he helped me up.

I watched as Tyler got in the guy's face. "You're my size, buddy. So why not talk your shit now?" Tyler dared him.

"Hey, what's going on?" another passerby asked as he approached with a friend. This time it was two black guys. I'd seen them around campus but I hadn't the slightest idea who they were.

"This asshole here was choking her, so I came over and stopped him," the white guy explained.

"Is that true?" one of the black guys asked Tyler. By this time, Tyler's boys joined him in the huddle. They stood there like they were Tyler's minions.

"Hey, Yoshi, are you all right?" Another voice rang in my ears. When I turned around to see who it was, I saw that it was Penny. She rushed to my side as I made my way away from the crowd that was rapidly growing.

"Come on, you guys, let's break this up," I heard through all the commotion. I refused to waste my time by looking back over my shoulder. That asshole Tyler had gotten enough of my time already.

"What happened?" Penny asked me after locking her arm into mine and walking with me to our dorm.

"Nothing." I brushed her question off.

"That's not what I saw. He assaulted you." Penny pressed the issue.

"He choked me," I clarified.

"Choke, shake, spit. It's all the same, which means that he assaulted you."

"Look, Penny, I am tired. I just lost my best friend and roommate. Her parents blame me for her death. They think that I gave her the drugs that she overdosed on, which is why they won't let me see her. I went to the hospital two hours ago and wasn't allowed to go into her room to say good-bye. Do you know how fucked up I felt to get escorted out of the hospital?"

"I'm sorry, I don't," she replied.

"Well, let me fill in the blanks for you. I felt like shit! I was embarrassed and mortified at how they talked to me in front of everyone that was there."

"I'm sorry to hear that." Penny held my arm a little tighter.

"Don't be sorry. It's not your fault. I've just gotta come to terms that everyone on this earth is not the same. We all think differently and we move differently."

"That's a good way of looking at it."

"I wonder how her parents will act if they see me at her funeral. Because I will be going, whether they like it or not."

"Wear a pair of black shades and a hat and you'll fit right in," Penny suggested. "I'll go with you if you like," she added.

"I really appreciate you offering. I'll let you know."

"Care to talk about what happened back there?" She got back on the issue dealing with Tyler assaulting me.

"It's nothing really." I once again tried to brush off the real reason why Tyler attacked me.

"You do know that you could press charges against him and issue a restraining order so that this incident never happens again?"

I sighed heavily. "Trust me, it's more complicated than that."

"I can keep secrets."

"I'm sure you can. But right now isn't a good time."

"Wanna talk about why you were out after midnight last night? From where I was sitting, it looked like you were running from someone."

"No, I wasn't running from anyone. I was rushing back to the dorm because I had to use the bathroom extremely bad."

"Are you sure that's why you were running to the dorm?"

"Yes, I am sure. And what's with all these questions? You're draining me out," I told her.

Penny looked surprised that I put her ass on the hot seat. I was sure she was concerned for my well-being, but she needed to dial it back a little. I couldn't deal with all that questioning. Had too much on my plate as it was.

"I'm sorry, Yoshi. But just know that any time you wanna talk and get some of that stuff off your chest, I'm right upstairs in dorm room 518."

"I appreciate that. Thank you," I said.

"Don't mention it."

Penny and I got on the elevator and pushed buttons for our respective floors. Before I exited the elevator, she reminded me that when I was ready to talk, she was the one to come to. I thanked her again and stepped out, and then the elevator doors closed.

Jessica came back to the dorm later that evening. I was there listening to music through my disc player and earphones when she walked into the room. Our eyes connected at once. I took the earphones off my ears and waited to hear what she had to say.

"They took Gia's body out of her room and transported it to the morgue," she started off. "Her parents said that they were going to figure out Gia's funeral arrangements and then let us know from there," she continued as she slumped down on her bed. Several seconds later, she took off her jacket and lay back on her bed. I watched her as she looked up at the ceiling but wouldn't say a word. But then I saw a couple of tears falling from her eye and down her temple, so I knew that she was coming to her breaking point.

I got up from my bed and walked over to hers. I sat down and started wiping the tears away from her eyes. From there, Jessica started crying uncontrollably.

"Yoshi, I can't believe that she's gone," she sobbed.

"I'm having a hard time believing it too," I consoled her.

"What are we gonna do now knowing that she's not coming back to this room?"

"I don't know, Jessica. I've been thinking about that since I left the hospital."

"It was fucked up how Gia's parents treated you today," Jessica said between the sobbing and the sniffling.

"It's not your fault. I guess what really matters is that Gia knows. Outside of that, I really don't care," I expressed. "Oh yeah, after I got on the elevator, her brother apologized to me for how his parents treated me outside Gia's room. He told me Gia said that I was her best friend and that she loved me a great deal, so hearing that made me feel so much better. I can honestly say that going up to the hospital was worth every insult and all the embarrassing comments Gia's parents made today."

"Well, I'm glad, because I was really worried about you after you left."

"You know me, Jessica. I'm a warrior," I assured her.

"I know you are," she replied.

We sat there next to each other in silence. I can't tell you what she was thinking about, but I can tell you my thoughts. The idea that Tyler threatened to kill me if I go around and say that he raped me was concerning. In fact, it was alarming. I didn't know much about this guy, but I knew that when I got up the gumption to make him pay for what he did to me, all hell would break loose.

While I thought about all the different scenarios that could happen when I blew the whistle on that guy, I became uncertain about doing it. Jessica was right. Why had I not gone to the freaking hospital? Why did I take that shower as soon as I got back to the dorm? But then again, why can't my word be good enough? I wouldn't walk around here and accuse a man of raping me if he hadn't. That's just not my character.

I Couldn't Believe My Eyes

The following day I got a call from Maria. I had just come back from Dunkin' Donuts with a cup of hot chocolate in my hand when my dorm room telephone started to ring. I placed my cup down on the desk and grabbed the cordless phone next to it.

"Hello?"

"Hey, Yoshi, I heard about Gia. How are you?"

"I appreciate you calling me," I commented, and then I took a sip of my hot chocolate.

"What are you doing now?"

"I just walked into my dorm room from Dunkin' Donuts."

"How is Jessica handling things?"

"She's still shocked by it. I'm sure it'll sink in sooner than later."

"I heard that Gia's parents are blaming you for her drug addiction."

I sighed heavily. "Who told you that?"

"Chelsea told me. She even told me that you went up to the hospital twice and that they wouldn't let you see her."

"Yeah, they didn't."

"Think they'll let you go to her funeral?"

"At this point, I really don't care, because I'm gonna go anyway."

"Yoshi, please don't do that. As much as it hurts, you gotta respect her parents' wishes and let them mourn her in their way."

"Easy for you to say because she wasn't your friend," I pointed out.

"No . . . it's easy for me to say because that's her family and you're an outsider."

"Maria, why do you always have to be so negative all the time? Nothing positive ever comes from your mouth when it pertains to Gia."

"That's because I knew what kind of person she was. Her parents knew that she was getting high, so she should've been woman enough to tell them that you had nothing to do with her addiction. But no, she let them believe what they wanted to believe and in turn hung you out to dry."

"Did you call me to start an argument?"

"No. I called you to check on you."

"Well then, let's talk about me."

"Is there something bothering you besides Gia's passing?" she asked me.

At one point, it felt like she had found out what happened to me at the frat house the other night. But then again, I felt that if she knew, she would've said something at the beginning of the conversation.

"The better question would be, what's not bothering me?" I made a general statement. I wasn't in the mood to talk about that. I figured I'd wait until she got back on campus before I offloaded all this bullshit on her. "It's that time of the month. You know how it is," I finally answered her.

"Okay, well stay out of trouble. And I'll see you in a couple of days," she mentioned.

"See you then," I said, and then we ended our call.

I hung out in my dorm room, listening to music and thinking about how things would be now that Gia was officially gone. To visualize it was hard. I didn't know what I would do without her. Despite what anyone says, she was ride or die and she will never be forgotten.

While I lay there in silence, Jessica called the room.

"Are you busy?" she immediately asked after I answered the cordless phone.

"No, why?"

"Gia's dad asked me to pack up her things and have them ready when he comes by today. But I won't be able to do it. I forgot that I had a hair appointment, so will you do it for me?"

"Jessica, you know that man hates my guts. I'm the last person he wants to see."

"You won't see him. After you pack up her stuff, take it to the first-floor office and he'll get it from there."

"What time is he supposed to come by?"

"In about two hours."

"Okay. I can take care of that."

"Cool! Thank you! Love you!"

"Love you too."

Packing up Gia's things seemed like a daunting task, but I set down the phone and went to work. Gia had three suitcases in her closet, so I grabbed them all. I placed the opened suitcases on her bed and pulled all of her clothes and shoes that were stored in there. I grabbed her underwear, lingerie, and toiletries from her storage bins and stuffed them in the suitcases as well. She only had a few photos lying around, so I slid them in a small pocket inside one of the suitcases. She had a storage bin underneath her bed, so I grabbed it and began emptying it out. In that bin, I found important documents like her birth certificate, her voter registration card, and life insurance declaration, among a few other things.

But what threw me for a loop was to find out that she had a diary, and there was no lock on it either. The curious person in me wanted to open it and read it. But the morally conscious person in me told me that it would not be nice to snoop in her business. Sorry to say, the curious person prevailed after reasoning that it wouldn't be wrong to go through it because she was no longer with us and I wouldn't be invading her privacy.

Before I cracked open Gia's diary, I finished packing her things and took them to the first-floor office.

"Sorry to hear about Gia," one of the dorm residents said after I closed the dorm office.

"Thank you. I appreciate you saying that," I replied, and made my way back on the elevator.

I couldn't have gotten to my floor fast enough. My curiosity was getting the best of me. It was fiending like a heroin addict looking for its next hit.

Immediately after I walked back into my room, I closed the door and locked it. I didn't want anyone walking in on me, realizing that I was reading Gia's diary. I suspected that Gia was going to talk about her breakup with her last boyfriend and of course about her drug habit. But to unravel more secrets blew my mind out into the universe.

Her first entry started off on July 6, 1992:

It's been two months now since Scott and I started dating, and we just had our first argument. In the beginning he used to tell me he loved me at least five times a day. He used to open and close my car door, bring me a red rose from the store when I used to make him run errands. But now, all that has stopped. He seems distant like he's not present. I ask him all the time have I done anything that would make him do a 180 on me, but he gives me the same answer and tells me no.

Tonight, I'm gonna go to his favorite Chinese spot and pick up some food and hopefully change his mood so he can stop being a grouch. I'll keep my fingers crossed.

The next entry was July 7, 1992:

Well, the Chinese meal didn't work. My pop-up to his apartment actually turned into a disaster. I had no idea that he was still entertaining his ex-girlfriend. She was at his freaking apartment washing her clothes. And when I asked him was he still sleeping with her, he told me no but they will always be friends and that he'll always have her back through any situation.

I just stood there not knowing whether to flip out on him or cry. If I would've cried then it would've looked like the girl won. So, instead of doing the latter, I held my head up and walked out of his apartment gracefully.

I thought he was going to call me after everything that transpired, but he didn't. When I heard from him again, two days had passed and I was the one that called him. I felt like shit. And in doing so, it made me look like I was running down behind him.

By the end of the call, I found myself begging him to give our relationship a chance. He agreed to do so and I was happy, even though I pressured him to do it.

The next twenty diary entries were also about her relationship problems with Scott. But in the thirteenth diary entry, I found out that Scott wasn't the only problem she had in her life. Federal agents were investigating her for wire fraud.

The entry was on August 11:

What the hell am I going to do? I allowed Scott to open a bank account in my name to use so that he and his friends could wire checks into. Now I've got the feds breathing down my throat. They paid me a visit today and asked me a slew of questions about the amounts of the checks and where they came from. They showed me screenshot amounts of $15,000, $7,200, $19,350, and the list goes on and on. They even had records that as soon as the checks were deposited, the funds were withdrawn. During the interview, I kept my cool. But after they left my dorm room, I was on the verge of having a meltdown. I immediately called Scott and briefed him about what happened and he acted like he didn't know what I was talking about. He literally acted like he didn't know what I was talking about. And to add insult to injury, he hung up on me. I called him back more than a dozen times but he refused to answer my call. I wanna tell both of my roommates about my dilemma, but all they'll do is ridicule me. I can hear Yoshi calling me stupid and remind me how she's been trying to get me to leave Scott because he's bad news. Jessica would tell me to rat him and his boys out and hang their asses out to dry. What am I going to do now?

Reading that entry made me both angry and sad because of the way Scott treated Gia and because Gia had to handle this ordeal by herself. Damn! I sure wished that she had shared this information with Jessica and me. Who knows? Things probably would've turned out differently.

Sitting in my room thinking about Gia's diary entries began to take a toll on me to the point that I had to go outside and get some fresh air. I didn't go far though. I sat on one of the picnic chairs in the area designated for smokers and watched the squirrels and birds roam around as they pleased.

A couple of my dorm residents spoke to me in passing and expressed their condolences. It felt good to know that Gia was known around campus because she was a good girl. Just a misguided person when it came to choosing the wrong people to be in her life.

While I sat there and reflected on Gia and what I read so far in her diary, my phone rang. I answered it on the second ring.

"Hi, Yoshi, it's your mother," I heard her say.

I was tempted to end the call, especially after all the horrible shit I heard her say about me before I left her home days ago, but then I thought that maybe she had something important to say. Like maybe apologize for being a bitch.

"Hello," I replied.

"Sydney mentioned that one of your roommates is in the hospital."

"Yes, she was in ICU in a medically induced coma and now she's dead."

"Oh my, I am sorry to hear that. Which roommate was it?"

"Gia. Gia Santos."

"I know that you must be taking it really hard."

"Yes, I am," I assured her.

"Is there anything that your stepfather and I can do to help you get through this ordeal?"

"I appreciate the gesture, but the only thing that would make me feel better is to have her here."

"How did she die?"

"She overdosed on drugs."

"Oh my God! No. She was on drugs?" My mother's voice pitch went up a couple of levels. "I know her parents are outraged. Did you know that she had a drug addiction?"

"Listen, Mom, I'm not in the mood to answer all of these questions. Just be happy that it's not me."

"Wait . . . wait a minute. . . . You use drugs too?" she asked me. I could hear the fear in her voice.

"Mom, listen, I'm fine. My other roommate, Jessica, is fine. But Gia isn't, so can we drop the subject?" I answered her without answering her question. I could tell that she was about to have a panic attack because she hates when she's not in control of something.

"Honey, if you have a drug problem, I could get you in a state-of-the-art outpatient substance abuse program."

"Mom, I told you that I was fine. Now, let's drop it," I demanded.

"Excuse me, are you Yoshi Lomax?" one of two white men asked. They were both wearing business casual jackets and blue and black pants.

"Mom, I gotta go. There's two guys standing in front of me and they want to talk," I said, and then ended our call. "Who wants to know?" I replied.

"I'm Detective Ranger, and this here is my partner, Detective Khols." One of them introduced both of them.

"What do you want with me?"

"We're investigating the death of your roommate, Gia Santos, and we want to ask you a few questions," Detective Ranger explained.

"Shoot. . . . I'm listening," I insisted.

"From our understanding, she ingested quite a few sleeping pills and cocaine and overdosed. So could you tell us where she got the drugs from?" Detective Ranger asked.

"No, I can't. Drugs are illegal, and especially on campus. And besides, how would I know when I was in New York visiting my parents?"

"We're aware that you were in New York while this unfortunate incident occurred. But at the same time, we were hopeful that you could give us any information that could lead to the arrest of her drug dealer," Detective Khols chimed in.

"Have you ever taken that same drug with Gia?" Detective Ranger asked.

"No," I replied. They could tell that I was aggravated with them.

"Would you submit to a drug test?" Detective Ranger added.

"No, I wouldn't. What'cha think I'm on probation or something? Ask me another question like that and I will end your fake-ass interrogation. You're treating me like I'm on trial or something. I'm studying law, so I know my fucking rights," I warned them.

"You don't have to get angry, Ms. Lomax. All we're trying to do is arrest the guy that sold your roommate the drugs and make him pay for her death. That's it," Detective Khols interjected.

"I told you I don't know the guy that sold her those drugs. Ask someone else that question. I'm sure they'll be able to help you," I suggested.

While answering the last questions these two cops had for me, Rita walked by and looked at us in a weird fashion. Detective Ranger noticed it too and called her out.

"Hey, excuse me, can I talk to you for a minute?" he yelled out.

Rita looked at him and then she looked back at me. "It's okay. I won't take up too much of your time. I just wanna ask you a couple of questions," he insisted.

Still hesitant, she stood there.

"I promise it'll only take two or three minutes. That's it," he assured her.

"Okay," Rita said, and then she waited for him to approach her. Meanwhile Detective Khols continued to question me.

"How was your relationship with Gia? Was Gia seeing someone? Had a boyfriend?" Detective Khols's questions continued.

"Not at the moment of her death. But she did have one."

"Do you know his name?"

"Yes, his name was Scott."

"Does this Scott have a last name?"

"I'm sure he does, but I don't know it."

"How was the relationship between Gia and your other roommate, Jessica?"

"If you're trying to imply that Jessica had something to do with Gia's overdose, then you're barking up the wrong tree. We treated one another like sisters and we looked out for each other. I was telling someone else that if I was here, Gia would not have taken those pills."

"Did Gia have any enemies?"

"Not to my knowledge. Everybody that knew her liked her," I expressed. I guess he felt like I had given him what he needed, so he thanked me for my time. He did hand me his card and encouraged me to call him if I thought of any other information later. After I assured him that I would, he bid me farewell and joined Detective Ranger and Rita.

I watched Rita as she tried to look confident, like she was controlling the conversation between her and the detectives. She looked at me a couple of times after she answered their questions. When the questioning was over, they handed her a business card and said good-bye.

"Thank you again for your time, Ms. Lomax," Detective Ranger said.

"Don't mention it." I gritted my teeth as they walked away.

"Yo, why they acting like somebody killed Gia? She overdosed, right?" Rita asked me after she took a seat in a chair next to me. She looked spooked.

"Yes, they know she overdosed. Now they want the person that gave her the drugs locked up," I explained.

"Wait, can they do that?" Rita asked. She looked petrified.

"Yes, they can do it."

"But she took the drugs on her own free will."

"I know. But Virginia code 18.2-248 says that it's illegal to sell or give a person drugs, and if it relates to their untimely death they could be charged with involuntary manslaughter and sentenced to a max of 40 years."

"When did they come up with that law?"

"While you were re-ing up with your connect," I replied sarcastically.

"Oh, so now it's my fault? Remember you and Jessica get high too," Rita pointed out to me.

"Don't remind me," I insisted and looked away from her.

I scanned the entire campus grounds around my dorm and watched students as they came and gone. I also wondered if they were getting high too. Rita wouldn't admit it, but she made a lot of money around here.

"Does your father know that you're selling drugs?" I added.

"What is that, a trick question? Where the fuck do you think I get 'em?"

"Don't let the cops find out," I warned her. But that didn't go over well with her.

She stood up from her seat and said, "You just make sure that you don't tell 'em, because I'll take you and a whole bunch of people down with me too."

"What is that, a threat?" I asked her.

"Take it any way you like," she told me, and then she strolled on inside my dorm.

When Duty Calls

I headed back to my room not too long after Rita and I had a few choice words for each other. The fact that she'd threaten me if I sold her out to the detectives didn't sit too well with me. I was appalled that she'd even think that I would rat her out in the first place. I don't want anyone to know about my bout with prescription drugs. I knew one thing: she better not come at me like that again or else.

Bored to death and needing something to take my mind off Tyler raping me, I decided to read more entries from Gia's diary. Her next entry was dated August 13.

Scott has had me so stressed out lately. Today when I called him, he wouldn't answer. I called him at least twenty times if not more and he'd send all my calls straight to his voicemail. I've texted him at least fifty times, asking him why he doesn't want to talk to me? I've done nothing wrong to him. All I've been was a loving and supportive girlfriend to him. I've bought him nice things, and I mean expensive things, hoping

he'll want to be around me, but that hasn't worked ei-
ther. Maybe I'm smothering him too much? Or maybe
he's going through something and wants to handle it
on his own? Whatever it is, I'm feeling the effects of it
as well.

The next diary entry was dated on the same night:

Scott finally answered my call and I was so happy.
He fussed at me for calling and leaving him all those
messages but I didn't care. All I wanted to do was hear
his voice, regardless of how he was speaking to me. In
the end, I won.

The next diary entry was on August 14.

I went over to Scott's place and caught him in the
bed with his ex. They were naked like they had just fin-
ished having sex and it hurt me to the core. I raised my
hand to hit her but Scott got between us. I was crying
my eyes out because he not only cheated on me, he de-
fended her. I swear, I cannot understand why this guy
treats me the way that he does.
After he put me out of his house, he called the cops
on me because I was making a scene outside his house.
The cops came and asked me to leave the property.
They even threatened to arrest me if I came back to
Scott's house. I was heartbroken and seriously
wondered how I was going to live without him. God,
why me? Why won't he love me?

Reading this entry from Gia's diary hit me hard. It sounded
like she was contemplating suicide right here on this day. I
am so angry that I didn't know what was going on with her.
This really hurt me to the core.

I was burned out from reading this last entry. To now know how Gia really felt in her last days was a wake-up call for me. But it was also sad. If only she had said something. Or gave Jessica and me a warning sign.

Right when I was closing up Gia's diary and sliding it underneath my pillow, Jessica walked into the room.

"Your hair looks good," I complimented her.

"Thank you," she replied as she closed the door. She slipped off her shoes and sat down on her bed. "What'cha been doing?"

"Just reading."

"Did you pack up all of Gia's things?"

"Yep."

"Did you get a chance to do it before her dad got here?"

"Yep."

"Good. Thanks."

"Two different detectives came here to talk to me today."

"What did they say?"

"They asked the same questions as the other two cops asked at the hospital. But these two want a name. They wanna know who Gia got her drugs from so they can charge them with manslaughter."

"No fucking way!" Jessica commented. She looked like a deer caught in the headlights.

"Yes way."

"Did you tell 'em?"

"Of course not. Are you crazy?"

"No, but you can't ever be too sure. That's why I asked you."

"Well, I will say this. From their mannerisms they aren't gonna stop until they find that person and make them pay for it."

"Does Rita know about this?"

"They talked to her too."

"No fucking way. How did that happen?"

"She was walking by while they were talking to me. So one of the detectives stopped her."

"What did they ask her?"

"They asked her the same questions that they asked me."

"What did she say?"

"I don't know. But after they left, she threatened to do something to me if I told them she was the connect."

Jessica's mouth opened this time. "Are you fucking kidding me?"

"Nope."

"Now when did she become so fucking tough? She's so freaking little. I could beat her ass if I wanted to."

"Maybe she got it from her father. Who knows? But I do know that I was out of town when all of this mess unfolded, and I will use that same alibi until this shit blows over," I expressed to Jessica. "Think the dean knows about Gia?" I changed the direction of the conversation.

"Oh, most definitely. Everything that happens on this campus, she knows about it."

"Well, why hasn't she showed her face around here?"

"Someone around here said that she and her family were in St. Barts somewhere."

"Well, that explains it."

"Have you eaten?"

"I haven't had much of an appetite."

"But you have to eat something."

"I know. I'll probably get a turkey sandwich from the dining room later."

"Have you seen Tyler since that party?" Jessica wanted to know.

"Have you talked to Conner?" I threw the question back at her.

"Yeah, I saw him a few minutes ago."

"What did he say to you?" I probed her.

"He just wanted to know had you talked to the cops, because you got people on campus thinking that Tyler raped you. I told him that you thought about going to the cops but that you hadn't done it yet."

"Jessica, are you fucking kidding me right now? Don't tell Conner anything else that we talk about! I don't want him in my freaking business," I roared.

"Why are you fussing at me? I didn't do anything wrong," she said, trying to play the victim.

"I'm fussing at you because you and I talked in confidence. If I wanted to tell Conner or Tyler what I am doing over here, then I would go over to the frat house and tell them myself. Just keep my name out of your mouth. Don't tell them shit else about me or what I'm over here doing."

"I'm sorry."

"Don't be sorry. Just be careful. Oh, and while we're on the subject, did that motherfucker tell you that he nearly choked me to death earlier today in the courtyard?"

"I heard something about that."

"Well, did you also hear that your boyfriend Conner mentioned that he wanted to fuck me?"

"What do you mean by that?" She got defensive. I could tell by her tone that she was feeling Conner more than she was letting on. This gave me a bad feeling.

"Just know that he said that he wanted to fuck me," I told her.

She hesitated for a moment like she was thinking. A few seconds later she said, "Yeah, he told me something like that. But he said that he was only playing."

"Jessica, Conner is lying to you. He and Tyler and some other guy heckled me like I was some trashy-ass one-night-stander."

"So, he did admit that you two had sex?"

"Yeah, he did. But he made it seem like it was consensual. But I shut his ass down and called him a fucking rapist."

"Out loud?"

"Yes, out loud, and he bum-rushed me. He grabbed me by my throat and lifted me up from the ground and told me that if I ever tell anyone that he raped me that he was going to kill me himself."

"Why the fuck is everyone threatening to kill you?"

"That's not the point, Jessica. That fucking bastard raped me, and when I called him out on it, he assaulted me."

"So what are you going to do?"

"I'm gonna press charges against him. That monster needs to be in jail. He can't go around putting hands on women, especially not me."

"You do know what's gonna happen if you do that?"

"At this point, I couldn't care less. I'm tired of men taking advantage of women. Using them for what they gain from them. Cheating on them with other girls, especially when you're giving them your all."

"Wait, you and he were in a relationship?"

"No, I'm speaking in a general sense. Men that bully women, whether it be physically, mentally, financially, or emotionally, they need to pay for it."

"I understand where you're going with this, but you should wait to run this by someone else. Maybe your best friend Maria. See what she says about it. And make sure you tell her that you took a shower so his DNA isn't on you, and also tell her that you two were seen kissing at his party that same night."

"I know Maria. She's gonna tell me to do it."

"Well then, there you go. But just wait on the backlash you're gonna get because of it. Tyler is a big deal around here, and no one is going to let you take him down without a fight."

Hearing Jessica tell me that I was about to get knee deep in some shit going after Tyler kind of weakened my confidence. But I couldn't let that deter me. If I did it, I could stop him from doing what he did to me to someone else. He was a monster, and I was gonna let everyone on this campus know it.

"Are you going to run for the hills when I expose his ass?"

"Of course not, you're my friend. Not him."

"Well, I wish you would act like it," I told her, and then I got up from my bed and left the room. I knew I needed to get away from her before I said something that I may regret later.

I had no idea where I was going when I left Jessica back in the room. I guess I just needed to blow off some steam. For a moment there, it sounded like she was on Tyler and his minions' side. And who cares about getting knee deep in shit. I was gonna make those weak-ass guys pay for what they did to me.

Who Else Want Some?

Two days went by and spring break was finally over, and an influx of students appeared everywhere. Some students were happy to be back on campus, and others weren't. Maria called me and told me that she was back and to meet her in the lobby of her dorm. I got there before she came down.

When she showed up a couple of minutes later, I stood up and gave her a tight hug, and then we sat down next to each other.

"So, tell me what's going on?" She didn't hold back. She wanted to get straight to the point.

"Where would you like me to start?" I asked, because I had a boatload of shit to tell her.

"How are you feeling now that Gia has passed away?"

"I feel empty. I feel sadness. I wish that I could've seen her or talked to her before she did what she did."

"You do know that it's not your fault, right?"

"Yes, I know that. But then something in the back of my head tells me that it is," I began to explain as my eyes started getting watery. I held my head back so the tears wouldn't fall, but my teardrops were too heavy.

Maria grabbed my hand and squeezed it lightly, and then she rubbed my back in a circular motion. This was her way of telling me that everything was going to be all right. "It's okay to cry," she insisted. "Have her parents reached back out to you yet? Maybe apologized for blaming you for her death?"

"No. But her brother told me that he knew that I didn't cause it. He even told me that Gia loved me like a sister," I replied, wiping away the tears from my face.

"See, that was nice. And how did that make you feel?"

"It made me feel good that someone in her family knew the truth," I said as I continued to dry the tears from my cheeks.

"Good. I'm glad he did that for you. Or else you'd be walking around here like a zombie, trying to cope with your loss," she added. "Has the dean talked to you yet?"

"No. She was on vacation with her family, but since the break is over, I'm sure she gonna call me into her office."

"Well, when she does, be straight with her."

"What? And tell her all the things that really happened in my room?"

"Yes, I don't see why not," Maria said candidly. But Maria lived in a fantasy world. She walked around with a picture in her mind of how everyone in the world should love one another; if you do someone wrong, apologize immediately; if you see someone hungry, feed them. I mean, I could go on and on, but I'm not that person. I'm vindictive. If you mess with me, you pay for it either now or later. Take your pick. And as for giving the dean a whole confession session, that wasn't gonna happen. No way, no how!

"I'm not at that stage in my life that I could be straight

up with everyone. If I was, then everyone in my life would hate me."

Maria chuckled. "How is Jessica taking it?"

"One day she's good and the next day she's not. I just let people mourn their loved ones on their own terms. She'll get past it when she's ready."

"What about you? How do you plan to get past it?"

"I'm not sure," I said, and then I hung my head low. When I lifted it back up, more tears formed in my eyes. "Something happened to me a few days ago and I'm trying to deal with it and trying to figure out to handle it, but I keep getting conflicting answers in my head," I added.

Maria gave me an alarming look. She tried to look me in the eyes, but I kept hanging my head low or looking in another direction. She grabbed me by my chin and forced me to look at her. "Tell me what happened?" she demanded.

I sat up straight, moving her hand from my face, and then I took a deep breath and exhaled. I thought for a moment, trying to figure out how to break the news to her, and then it came to me.

"Jessica and I went to a frat party the other night. She thought that it would be good for us to hang out and get a breather because of all the stuff that was going on with Gia. So, Tyler and his friends—"

"Tyler the football player, right?" She cut me off.

"Yes, that one," I answered. "So when he and his friends saw me and Jessica, they greeted us, gave us drinks. Then we went into heavy dialog about school, why either of us had girlfriends and boyfriends. What's our favorite food. Whatever you can think about, that's what we talked about. So, anyway, as the night went on, the more and more time Tyler and I spent together, he started moving closer to me, and then before I knew it, we had started kissing. Now mind you, everyone at the party sees us. The girls that were there turned their noses at me. But that didn't concern me. I was having fun, and for that moment that time took my mind off Gia being in the hospital. So now Tyler suggests that we should go upstairs to his room so we can have alone time. I agree to it and we leave."

"Where was Jessica when this was happening?"

"She was on the other side of the living room entertaining one of Tyler's frat brothers."

"Okay, continue . . ."

"So, when we got upstairs, we sat on his bed and started talking more. We started kissing again and then three minutes into it, he starts taking off his pants. I'm looking at him asking him what is he doing? He ignores me and climbs on top of me. And I'm resisting, telling him to get off me. He's not listening and begins to take off my pants. I'm pushing him back and demand that he stop and that I'm not sleeping with him. But once again, he's not listening. So I try to kick him in his dick and miss it, and from there he went off. He hits me in the face and then he rapes me," I explained, and then I started bawling my eyes out.

Maria sat there, looking more horrified than anything. "Tyler raped you?" she finally said.

"Yes," I replied, wiping my eyes and face.

"Did you report it to the police?" she asked as she slid closer to me.

"No."

"Why not?"

"Because I wasn't thinking straight."

"What do you mean by that?"

"When he got off me, I grabbed my pants and ran out the frat house. And when I got back to my room, I took a shower. I erased all his DNA off me."

"Where was Jessica when this was going on?"

"She had already left the party."

"Does she know about this?"

"Yes, I told her the next morning."

"Did you get a rape kit from the hospital?"

"No," I said, still sobbing my eyes out. It seemed like the more questions Maria asked me, the more I looked like an idiot.

"Yoshi, come on. You know better than that," Maria stated as she embraced me.

"I know. I know. And that's why I'm so angry with myself."

"Have you seen Tyler since this happened?"

"Yes."

"Did he say anything to you?"

"Yes."

"Where were you guys at and what did he say?"

"He and his boys were passing me by in the middle of the court grounds, and Tyler shouted comments about when was I coming to see him again. I kiss good and the sex was good. And then his friends started heckling me too, asking me when was I coming to see them. It was humiliating, so I fired back at them and yelled that Tyler raped me. And in a matter of three seconds he ran to me, grabbed me by my throat, and lifted me up from the ground and threatened to kill me if I ever say that again."

"And what did you do?"

"I was gasping for air, trying to get him to release me because I couldn't breathe."

"Did anyone else see this?"

"Yes, a few guys stopped and intervened. There's a girl that lives in my building named Penny, and she stopped and helped me too."

"Does she know that he raped you?"

"No, I didn't mention it."

"Yoshi, we've gotta figure something out. That fucking rapist needs to pay for what he did to you."

"I know. And I wanna press charges, but Jessica said that since I don't have the rape kit DNA results and a witness, then I don't have a case."

"I hate to say this, but she's right. No one at that party is going to corroborate your story. For all they know, you two had consensual sex, especially since you and he showed a public display of affection before that incident happened."

"So I should just give up and let him get away with it?"

"No, I'm saying that you need to talk to someone. Go and see a lawyer. Tell him what you told me and go from there."

"Will you go with me?" I asked her. I knew that I didn't want to go at this alone. I needed someone to be by my side, and I knew that Maria would be that perfect someone.

"Absolutely," Maria assured me.

Hearing her tell me that she would accompany me when I go and speak with an attorney meant the world to me. I wished that Gia was here too, because I knew that she would've stepped up to the plate before I would've even asked Maria to go. That's just how solid my relationship was with Gia. She'd go to hell and back if I asked her to. Damn! I'm gonna miss that girl.

"You know homicide detectives are trying to pin Gia's murder on someone?" I changed the subject.

"What do you mean?" Maria wanted to know.

"They stopped by here and asked me if I knew the dealer that sold Gia those drugs," I replied.

"What did you say?"

"I told them that I didn't know."

"But you do know, right?" Maria pressed me.

"Of course I do."

"So why didn't you tell 'em?"

"And have my head on a chopping block the very next day? No, thank you!"

"Did they search you guys' room?"

"No, I don't think so."

"Did they ask?"

"Maybe they asked Jessica, I don't know. Remember I was in New York."

"Did they ask you if you took drugs?"

"No."

"What about Jessica?"

"I don't know. I mean, if they did, she didn't mention it. And what's up with all these questions, Maria?" I got aggravated. All I wanted to do was get her take on if the cops could try and implicate me in Gia's overdose. That's it. I didn't need the third degree. "Look, I'm gonna head back to my dorm. I'm glad you got back safely. I'll get with you tomorrow," I continued, and then I stood up from my seat.

"I love you," she said as I walked away.

"I love you too," I replied without looking back. The thing is, I know Maria loves me. She just has this crazy and militant way of showing it. She's more like a hard-nose-ass boot-camp instructor who has your best interest at heart but doesn't want to show it. She's pretty weird at times, but she's loyal and that's why she's my best friend.

Double Trouble

The following day, the dean called me and asked me to come to her office at one p.m. to discuss what happened to Gia during the break. Dean Paige was a stuffy, old Hillary Clinton look-alike. She was always politically right about everything. Everything had to go by the book. You had to dot all your i's and cross all your t's. She was so annoying. So I knew this meeting with her was going to be the exact same way.

"Come on in, and have a seat right there," she instructed me. If you ever been inside of a probation officer's office, then this place looked just like it. Family pictures of the spouse and the kids on vacation in Australia, at snow resorts in Aspen, fishing and kayaking at a campsite. Sorority member plaques; bachelor, master, and doctorate degrees of education, psychology, and behavioral science; award plaques for high achievement and volunteer work. This lady had seen and done it all, so if I came in there with some bullshit, she would spot it before I opened my mouth.

I sat down in a seat directly in front of her desk and acted like I was admiring all her degrees on the wall.

"Are you comfortable?" she asked me.

"Yes," I replied, giving her a nervous expression.

"I called you in here to talk about Gia Santos and get your side of what happened in your dorm room," she announced.

"I really don't have much to say because I was in New York visiting my family. But when I got a phone call that she was rushed to the hospital, I came back the next day," I began to explain.

"Did you know that she had a drug habit?" the dean asked me. And when I tell you she was eyeing me down, believe it. It felt like she was tossing test questions at me to get a feel for my answers and my body language.

"I've seen her taking a couple of pills here and there. But it wasn't to the point of her overdosing."

"What do you mean by that?"

"She used to get migraines. So when she took a pill here and there, I figured she was going to fight back her migraine headaches," I lied. But I knew I was convincing because the dean asked her next question.

"Was she depressed?"

"Not to my knowledge," I lied once again.

"What about your other roommate?"

"What about her?"

"Does she use prescription pills?"

"Not to my knowledge. If she does, then she's doing it somewhere else."

"Why do you say that?"

"Because she's never around. She's always in the library, study groups, and doing volunteer work for a literacy organization that she's a part of," I lied once more. This lying thing was becoming easier with each lie I told.

"Do we have a drug dealer on campus?" the dean asked me point blank.

Shocked by her blatant way of questioning me, I hesitated

for a moment because I didn't think that she'd be so bold. "Not to my knowledge," I finally answered her.

"If there were, would you tell me?" she pressed me.

Now this was a trick question. See, if I tell her that I would tell her that there was a drug dealer on campus, then she'd know that I was lying. But if I played reverse psychology with her and told her that I wouldn't tell her if I knew that there was a dealer on campus, then I knew that she'd believe me. So that's what I did.

"No disrespect to you, ma'am, but no I wouldn't tell you," I finally said.

"While I don't like your answer, I admire you for your honesty," she told me. "Now there will be an investigation conducted, so if there is a drug dealer on our campus, they will be arrested and dealt with to the fullest extent of the law. Just like our missing student, Kristen Chambers. I'm deeply troubled that we haven't been able to find her. Her parents call me or the missing person's unit at least once a week to check on the status of the investigation. But unfortunately, we haven't had anything new to tell them. It saddens me when these types of things are happening on my campus. Old Dominion University is a well-respected, vibrant, and diverse campus. We embrace our diversity and ensure that we strive toward creating an inclusive and welcoming community. We have a long and proud legacy of commitment to the principles of equality and equal opportunity for all students, faculty, and staff. We have made the commitment to provide a high quality of education to all of our students so that they may excel here and after they have gone on to their prospective careers. And to do so, it is our duty to enforce the rules of this university."

"Trust me, I understand perfectly," I assured her.

"Well, good. I'm glad. So what I want you to do is keep your ears and eyes open. And if anything sticks out to you that may help the investigators, let me know at once. Now, can you do that?"

"Yes, ma'am, I can."

"Is there anything that you need? We have an onsite chaplain if you need to talk. We also have a couple of counselors onsite whom you could talk to and could help you cope with the loss of your roommate," she offered.

I wanted to tell her that their prize football player raped me the other night. But I knew she wouldn't have believed me. She'd probably give me the same spiel everyone else has told me. When you don't have the DNA, you don't have a case. Instead, I told her that I appreciated the gesture and thanked her.

"Here, take these two cards," she insisted, and handed me two business cards she pulled out of one of her desk drawers. "One card is for Dr. Wingate. He's scheduled to be on campus Mondays, Wednesdays, and Thursdays. Mr. Blanchard's schedule is Tuesdays, Thursdays, and Fridays. He's on campus for half days on Saturdays. So give them both a call, and you can decide," she continued.

"I will, and thank you," I said, and stood up from the chair.

She walked around her desk and escorted me to her office door. "Remember to keep your eyes and ears open and let me know if you hear anything, okay?"

"Okay," I replied, and then left.

You Have No Idea

There was a message left for me from Benny Shaw, Esq., on the dorm room telephone asking to call him back. He was a defense attorney and specialized in criminal and family law. From the looks of his resume, he definitely had his finger on the pulse of the Commonwealth of Virginia law, because he had won a lot of cases. I called him earlier and he was returning my call, so I called him back.

"Hello, Yoshi, how can I help you?" he started off.

"Hi, Mr. Shaw. I just have a couple of questions that I wanna run by you and hopefully you can help me."

"Okay, shoot."

"I'm a college student at ODU, and a few days ago I went to a frat party. At the party I hung out with a popular football player. We had several drinks, we talked, and then he suggested that we go upstairs to his room. So I obliged—"

"I know where this goes . . ." the attorney interjected.

His cutting me off midsentence almost made me want to disconnect our call. It was humiliating enough that I had to go into detail about what Tyler had done to me.

"Go on," he insisted as if I was taking up his precious time.

"After I agreed to go upstairs with him, we went in his room, sat down on his bed, and then he started kissing on me. The kissing was fine. But when he started pushing it further by taking off his pants and then trying to undress me, I wanted him to stop."

"Did you tell him to stop?"

"Yes, I did."

"And what did he do?"

"He kept pursuing me. I tried to push him off me. I told him to stop, but he wouldn't listen."

"What happened next?"

"He pulled his penis out of his underwear and tried to stick it in me. So I tried to kick it, but I missed and kicked him in the stomach instead, and he went berserk on me and hit me twice in my face and told me if I did it again that he was going to kill me."

"Did he rape you after that?"

"Yes, he did."

"Did you report it to the police?"

"No."

"Why not?"

"Because I was told that I waited too late."

"Who told you that?"

"My roommate."

"Did you go to the hospital and have them perform a rape kit?"

"No. When I ran out of the party, I went straight back to my dorm and took a shower. I felt dirty and I wanted to get his smell off me."

"While I understand your reasoning for your actions, you have to have proof that you've been raped. And the fact that you no longer have his DNA inside of you means this won't hold up in court."

"So that's it?"

"Did anyone see him rape you?"

"No. We were alone in his room."

"You said that you were at a party. Do you think that you could get one of the other guests to be a character witness. I mean, who knows? He may have done it to someone else. And if that's the case, then you two could file a joint claim."

"That'll never happen. He's a god on campus."

"I'm not too sure if that'll work, but run your story by one of the Special Victims Unit detectives down at the Eighth Precinct and see what they say."

"Is there any particular detective I should ask for?"

"No. Just talk to whoever is available."

"Okay. Thank you."

"Good luck," he said, and ended our call.

Feeling an overwhelming amount of defeat, I headed outside and sat on the nearest bench. The fact that every door I approached was being shut in my face was crushing me on the inside. Was I supposed to let that bastard rape me and then let him get away with it? That's not how life goes. You can't do something to someone and expect not to pay the consequences. Tyler had to pay for what he did to me. And he would as long as I had air in my body.

I got teary-eyed a few times, thinking about how fucked up my life was. I realized that I had spoken to everyone but my mother, so I willed myself to dial her number and get her on the phone, because this time I needed her. She answered my call on the second ring.

"Hello," she said.

"Hi, Mom," I replied.

"Hi, Yoshi," she said. Her words sounded stale.

"Mom, I really need to talk to you."

"What is this about, Yoshi?"

"Will you just listen to what I have to say first?"

"Go on."

"Mom, I went to a party a few days ago and was raped by one of the guys of a fraternity. After he raped me, I ran out of the house with my pants in my hand and went to my dorm and took a shower. I didn't go to the emergency room and get rape tested. I saw the guy who raped me the next day, and he heckled me around a group of people on campus, saying that I gave him good sex and that I can kiss. While he was doing that, I accused him of raping me in front of those same people. And when I did that, he grabbed me around my neck and started choking me to the point that I couldn't breathe. He even threatened to kill me if I ever repeated that he raped me. But at this point, I don't care what happens to me. I want to report him to the police, but as it stands I may not have a case against him. So what do you think I should do?"

Before I realized it, tears started rolling down my face. She couldn't see it, but I was sure that she heard my sniffles through the phone.

"Are you sure he raped you?"

"Of course, Mom, you know me. You know I wouldn't make up nothing about that."

"Well, whoever told you that you should've gotten a rape kit was right."

"So what do I do? Just let him get away with it?"

"Was he a white guy or black?"

"What does it matter, Mom?"

"It makes a lot of difference."

"Well, he was white."

"Oh well, you can forget it. Now that judicial system down in Virginia isn't gonna take the word of a black and Asian woman that she was raped by a white boy. And especially if you don't have the results of a rape kit."

"What about the fact that he said that he'd kill me? He literally threatened to inflict bodily harm on me."

"Yoshi, you don't have a case. They aren't gonna take your word over his. So drop it."

"What the hell is wrong with you? You're so negative all the time. You never have my back on anything." I sobbed louder. At this point, I didn't care who heard me crying. I was hurting on the inside and I had to let it out.

"Yoshi, let's face it. You're living in the real world, honey. Everything isn't gonna be perfect all the time."

"Look, Mom, just stop it, will you? Just be quiet. You've said all that I needed to hear right now."

"So what are you going to do?"

"None of your fucking business," I roared through clenched teeth, and then I ended our call.

The Eighth Street Precinct

I could punch myself for going to my mother thinking that she could help me out with my situation. If I didn't have to purchase another telephone for our room, I would've smashed it into the wall. Instead, I got up the gumption to go to the cops. I figured if no one else believes me, then the cops will.

I called a taxi instead of getting one of my friends on campus to drop me off at Eighth Street. As I walked toward the front entrance, anxiety began to take over my entire stomach. From there, it formed into a ball and started turning in circles like a hamster on a wheel.

While I was walking into the building, a white cop was exiting and held the door open for me so that I could enter. "Thank you," I said.

"You're quite welcome, ma'am," he replied.

As I crossed over the threshold, I realized that the room was a tiny fifteen-by-twenty-foot space with a small glass partition and a woman standing behind it. A metal door was next to it. I figured that was where the cop had exited. The walls were made of gray cinder block, and the floors were made of industrial-style epoxy like you'd see in prisons.

"Can I help you?" a full-figured Hispanic woman around forty asked me from the other side of the glass.

"I need to speak with a detective in the Special Victims Unit," I replied.

"What is your name and the nature of this visit?"

"My name is Yoshi Lomax and I was raped and I want to make a report," I said quietly, as if I was ashamed that someone was going to hear me. But I was alone and the woman saw that too.

"It's okay, ma'am. You're fine. No one is going to hurt you here," she assured me, and it felt good to hear those words. "Take this clipboard and fill out as much as you can, and I will have a detective come out and see you momentarily." She handed me the clipboard and a black-and-white form attached to it.

I took the clipboard and sat down in one of the five chairs placed in the room. It was a Q&A form asking for the date, time, and location of the rape. I had to give the perpetrator's full name, his physical address if applicable, his personal description, as much detail of the incident I could muster up, and then it asked for the time and location where the rape kit was performed. Once again, I felt a blow of defeat hitting me in the gut. I didn't have that information to add to this form. So what was I going to do now?

After I filled out as much as I could, I sat there and waited to be called. Thirty minutes passed, and I was still sitting in the same spot. I was somewhat nervous, but I was also bored. I wished that this would hurry up and go. But that didn't happen. Another fifteen minutes passed, and I was still a sitting duck. To help the time pass by, I got on the pay phone located on the wall a few feet away from me. I called the phone in my dorm room and hoped that someone would answer.

"Hello," I heard Jessica say. Hearing her voice was like music to my ears.

"Hey, girl," I greeted her back.

"Where are you?" she wanted to know.

"At the Eighth Precinct police station."

"Why didn't you tell me so that I could've gone with you?" she asked me.

"Because I did it at the last minute," I replied, trying to talk as low as I could.

"Have you seen a cop yet?"

"No, I'm waiting for one to call me now."

"Have you been crying?"

"What kind of question is that, Jessica? So what is going on?"

"Dean just called and told me to come to her office."

"She called me into her office earlier," I whispered into the phone while partially covering up my mouth.

"What did she say?"

"I can't get into that right now. I'll be on this phone for the next hour talking about it and I don't have that much time."

Before Jessica could respond, my attention was redirected after hearing my name.

"Are you Yoshi Lomax?" asked a white cop in plain clothes standing in the doorway.

"Yes, I am," I answered. "I gotta go," I told Jessica, and then I ended our call without giving her time to say another word to me.

I walked through the door that he held open for me. He instructed me to follow him, so I did. I followed him to a conference room with a glass door only twenty feet away. There was a long executive-style conference table placed in the middle of the floor and eight chairs surrounding it.

"Hand me the clipboard with your form and take a seat anywhere you like," he instructed me.

I sat down in a chair next to the door of the room. He sat down in a seat across from me. I watched him as he reviewed the questions that were printed and the answers I added to the form.

"Your name is Yoshi Lomax?" he asked me after taking his eyes away from the form.

"Yes, sir," I replied.

"My name is Detective Easton, and I will be recording and taking notices from your claim, so I want you to be truthful and as transparent as you can. Now, can you do that for me?" He pulled out a black voice recorder from his back pocket and a white legal pad from underneath the clipboard I had just handed him.

"Yes, I can," I assured him.

"Okay, so let's start off with your name, today's date, where you live, what you're here for, and the name of the accused."

I knew that I was nervous when my throat got dry after he asked me the first question. The fact that he was recording my story made it feel as if there was no turning back. I was here and now all the cards would be laid out on the table.

"My name is Yoshi Lomax, today is April 10, I attend Old Dominion University, and I am here to report a rape."

"What's the name of the accused?"

"Tyler Egan."

"Can you tell me how you know the accused?"

"Yes, he's the quarterback football player of the ODU Monarchs."

"Was this an isolated incident?"

"You mean was this the only time he raped me?"

"Yes."

"Yes, it was."

"So you're saying that this was the first time you two met?"

"No, I'm saying that I know him from his playing football but this was the first and only time that we spent time with each other," I clarified.

"Okay, now tell me what happened. And speak clearly so that the recorder can pick up every word you say."

"All right," I said, and then I paused to gather my thoughts. "My roommate, Jessica, invited me to go with her to a frat party on campus. So I agreed and we left."

"What time did you get there?" the detective asked me.

"Maybe a little after nine."

"Who let you in the house?"

"One of the frat boys let Jessica and me into the house."

"What did you do after that?"

"We were approached by Tyler Egan and another guy. The guy asked if we wanted drinks. We said yes and the guy got them for us."

"What kind of drinks?"

"I had beer and Jessica had tequila."

"What happened after that?"

"I took a seat on a sofa, Tyler took a seat beside me while my roommate Jessica and the other guy sat down on a couch across from us."

"Continue…"

"Well, things were cool for about the first couple of hours. We talked, we were laughing and drinking and stuff."

"Were you drunk?"

"I wouldn't say that I was drunk, but I was buzzing a bit."

"I don't know what that is. Explain it to me."

"My definition of drunk is when you drink alcohol to the point where you're debilitated. I was tipsy, which means that I was buzzing but I was fully coherent to make wise and rational judgment calls, which was what I did at the party before Tyler raped me."

"OK, slow down. We'll get to that point in a minute. So you're telling me that you were fully coherent?"

"Yes, that's exactly what I am saying."

"So what happened after the talking, laughing, and drinking?"

"Well, we kissed a few times."

"Was he a good kisser?"

"At that time, he was."

"Okay, so continue."

"Well, after we kissed for a while, he suggested that we go to his room where it was quieter and could talk better instead of yelling our words over the loud music that was being played by the deejay."

"Did you take him up on it?"

"Yes."

"And what happened after that?"

"After we went into his room, we sat down on his bed. We did a little talking and then we started kissing. I was fine with kissing him, but after about two to three minutes of that he decides that he wants sex."

"Did he tell you that he wanted to have sex?"

"No, but when I saw him taking off his pants, it couldn't have meant anything else."

"Explain yourself. Give me more details."

"When he started taking off his pants, I asked him what was he doing. And he said that he was going to give me what I've been waiting for. So I told him that I wasn't waiting for anything. But he ignored me and started pulling my pants off my body. I started kicking at him, telling him to stop and that I didn't want to have sex with him."

"How many times did you tell him to stop?"

"At least a dozen if not more."

"What happened after that?"

"After he snatched my pants off, he climbed on top of me, pulled his penis out, and then he tried to aim it so that he could put it inside of me, but I kicked him."

"Where did you kick him?"

"I kicked him in his stomach, but I tried to aim my foot at his groin area."

"What did he do after you kicked him?"

"He backhandedly smacked me twice in my face and threatened to kill me if I did it again."

"What happened next?"

"I didn't kick him anymore, but I started crying and begging him to get off me. But he wouldn't."

"Did he penetrate you with his penis?"

"Yes, he pushed himself inside of me and didn't stop until he was done."

"How did you get out of his bedroom?"

"After he rolled off me, I grabbed my pants and ran out."

"Of his room?"

"Yes."

"Where did you go?"

"I ran down the flight of stairs and out of the frat house."

"Who all was there?"

"Where?"

"Who witnessed you running out of the frat house carrying your pants in your hands?"

"There were only a few people there when I left."

"Where was your roommate?"

"She had already left."

"What was the name of the hospital that took your exam?"

"I didn't go."

"You didn't go to the hospital?"

"No."

"So what did you do after you left the frat house?"

"I ran back to my dorm and took a shower. I felt really sticky and dirty and had to get his smell off me."

"Do you have your undergarments? Like say, your panties? Something that we could get his DNA from?"

"I think my roommate took them and trashed them."

"You do know that if you don't have this guy's DNA, the rape exam, or a witness who saw him rape you, it will be hard to charge and convict this guy. Unless he makes a confession. And I doubt that he'll do that."

"So what's gonna happen now?"

"I can file the rape allegation and get one of our guys to investigate it, but that's all I can say right now."

"What if my roommate didn't throw away my panties? Can I bring them in as proof?"

"Of course, bring them in. But it won't seal his fate."

"Why not?"

"Because he can say that you and he willingly had consensual sex. Unfortunately, it would be your word against his."

"That fucking bastard," I said, folding my hand into a fist and slamming it on the table in front of me. "Do you know that I saw him and his friends the very next day? He had them laughing at me, talking about how good they heard my sex was and that they wanted me next. Do you know how upset and hurt I felt when I heard that?"

"I'm sure it was humiliating, but what that sounds like to me is he looks at that night as a one-night stand and not a rape."

"Well, it wasn't a one-night stand!" I shouted. My heart began to break into little pieces while suffering a major blow of anxiety.

"Ms. Lomax, I know you're upset, but I'm afraid that you're gonna have to calm down," he said mildly.

But it didn't help much, because my eyes filled up with tears and then there was an overflow. He grabbed a tissue box from a small table behind us and handed it to me.

I took one of the tissues from the box and began to wipe the tears from my eyes. While I was doing so, he pressed the red button to end the voice recorder.

"I'm sorry that you're upset, Ms. Lomax, but we've got to follow the law. Now let me get this information to one of my detectives, and they'll be getting in touch with you soon. In the meanwhile, if you find your underwear, put it in a Ziplock bag and drop it off at this office. Understand?"

"Yes, I understand," I replied between sniffles while I continued to dry my face with the tissue.

"Come on, I can walk you back to the exit door," he offered as he stood up from his chair.

I stood up too and followed him out of the conference room. When we approached the exit door, he opened it and let me out. "Have a nice day," he said.

"Yeah, you too," I said without looking back at him.

What Will It Take?

I thought that Jessica would be in our dorm room when I returned but she wasn't, so I climbed into my bed and tried to take a nap. I figured since I had nothing else to do, why not get some Zzz's to take my mind off everything that was going on. Now I couldn't say that taking a nap would help my situation, but it was worth a try.

I sleep better when I lay on my stomach, so I turned over. I even turned my closed eyes away from the window to block the sunlight that was shining through the mini blinds. For the first fifteen minutes, what I was doing felt like it would work, but for some reason I couldn't get myself to fall asleep. This would be one of those times that I needed a Vicodin. If I had at least half a pill, I would be good. Too bad, Gia used all the ones she had stashed away. If she hadn't, I would be able to wind down and she would still be alive.

With no other remedy in sight, I sat up in my bed and grabbed Gia's diary from underneath my mattress. I skimmed through a few pages that talked more about how badly her ex-boyfriend treated her and the deep hole she was sinking into. It became apparent that he was a serial cheater and he was vocally disrespectful. But when I read in another entry what he did to her, I wanted to hunt down his ass.

This entry was written on August 20, 1992.

Scott and I got into another fight tonight. I saw him on campus standing outside the food court talking to yet another girl. I asked him where was his ex-girlfriend? And did she know that he was creeping with another girl? He tried to brush me off by trying to ignore me. He even instructed her to walk with him to get away from me. But I followed him everywhere he went. And when he got sick of me doing it, he turned around, walked towards me and then he spit in my face. I was mortified. And what was even crazier was that when he walked back to where she was standing and asked her to continue following him, she did. Do you know that if I was with a guy that spits on another woman's face in front of me, I would try to get away from him as far as I could? I would even lose his freaking phone number. But never mind her, this motherfucker spit in my face and all I did was stand there and watch him as he walked in the opposite direction of me. I swear, I didn't know what on earth to do. So, I sat there heartbroken and cried alone.

Jessica finally came back to the dorm, and when she started to enter the room, I was reading Gia's diary but I put it away as she opened the door fully. She looked flustered as she came in with a fast-food bag from McDonald's.

"You will not believe the day I've had," she started saying as she slid off her hot-pink shoes and sat down on her bed.

"What happened?" I asked her, trying to look formal like I hadn't just read an entry in Gia's diary.

"First I went to my hair appointment and that turned out to be a disaster because the girl didn't do what I told her to do. Look at it, it's a fucking mess," she said as she pointed to the side views of her hair. "And then as soon as I walk into this room, I get a call from the dean asking me to come and see her. Actually, that's right before you called me. I wanted to ask you for a heads-up on the questions that she would ask me, but that didn't happen because you had to go into the police station."

"Did you see her?" I interjected.

"Yes, I saw her."

"What did she say?'

"She wanted to know where I was before the incident with Gia happened. So I told her. Then she asked me was Gia depressed? And I told her that I didn't think she was. Then she asked me if Gia was on prescribed muscle relaxers? I told her that I wasn't sure. Then she wanted to know if Gia had an addiction to drugs? And I told her that I wasn't aware of it."

"Why didn't you just say no?" I spat.

"I don't know, Yoshi. That answer just popped out," Jessica tried to explain.

"Did she ask you about me? If I was on drugs too?"

"Yes, she asked me that, and I told her no."

"What else did she say?"

"She asked me if Gia had a boyfriend at the time of her suicide, and if so, how was their relationship? If it was toxic. Because if it was, then that could've been her reason for committing suicide."

"What did you tell her?"

"I told her that I thought that her relationship was like any other. They had their problems. They work them out and then they either stay together or separate."

"Is that it? Is that all she asked you?" I pressed her.

Jessica sat there for a moment like she was jogging her memory. She looked at me and then she looked up to the ceiling. The second she looked back at me, she said, "Oh yeah, she just told me that if I hear anything concerning Gia to let her know."

"That's it?"

"Yeah, that's it," she assured me. "How did everything go at the police station? Were you able to file charges against Tyler?"

"What did you do with my clothes on the night of that party?" I asked, turning the question back to her.

"What are you talking about? I didn't see your clothes."

"I put them in a clear trash bag and threw them in the trash behind the bathroom door."

"If you put them there, then they're in the dumpster outside the building. You know I take the trash out when I leave for my first class in the morning."

"Fuck! Has the dumpster been emptied yet?"

"What are you talking about, Yoshi. That was four days ago, so you know the trash truck has been here at least twice, if not more. The cops need that bag, huh?"

"Yes, and I can't believe that I threw it in the trash."

"What did the cops say?"

"A white guy that took my report said the same thing that everybody else said. I should've gotten a rape kit performed on me, and the fact that the other people in the house saw Tyler and me kissing each other, it would be hard to get the charges to stick."

"Well, is he going to charge him with it?"

"He said that he's gonna file the report and that a detective will be assigned to the case and from there he will conduct an investigation."

"Did he say who the detective would be?"

"Nope."

"Don't worry. Everything's gonna be all right."

"I hope so, because I'm not going to be able to walk around on this campus and see him go on with his life like everything is cool. No, it's not cool and I'm gonna make sure he gets what comes to him."

"I don't blame you," Jessica commented.

"Heard anything about Gia's funeral?"

"Oh yeah, so her service is Saturday, which is two days from now, and it's gonna be in Virginia Beach at a church called The Rock church. It's on Witchduck Road."

"What time?"

"Two o'clock."

"Have you viewed her body yet?"

"No. That's gonna take place the night before her funeral."

"Where?"

"At Mane Clark's Funeral Home. I was told that it wasn't that far from the church."

"Are you going?"

"To view her body?"

"Yeah."

"Yes, I'm going. Why, you wanna go with me?"

"Of course I do."

"Well, please make sure you wear sunglasses, because from what I heard, Gia's mother really doesn't want you to be there."

"But why?" I shouted to the ceiling in my room. I know every resident on the same floor, above me, and below me heard my voice.

"Yoshi, you already know why. And I really don't wanna have this conversation, because I know that it hurts you that her parents don't want you around. They could easily blame me for her death, but they choose you instead and it's not fair."

"Yes, exactly," I said, and started sobbing my eyes out all over again. "Why won't they get it in their brain that I wasn't around. I was in New York visiting my dysfunctional-ass mother."

"I know, Yoshi, I know," Jessica said peacefully as she slid off her bed and then got on mine. "Maybe if I pull the dad to the side and talk to him, he'll see things from our perspective."

"It's not gonna work and you know it."

"We won't know unless I try it."

"Just forget it. All that matters is that Gia knew I loved her."

"That's a good way of looking at it," Jessica commented. She rubbed her hand across my back.

"Had Gia ever talked to you about how much of a dickhead her ex-boyfriend was?" I asked, abruptly changing the subject.

"Sometimes, why?"

"Because he was a fucking idiot. And he might've been the reason why she took all those fucking pills," I said through clenched teeth.

"I kind of figured as much."

"Has he reached out to you? I'm sure he knows about Gia's death, but has he reached out to you or her family so that he could attend the funeral?"

"No, he hasn't reached out to me. But didn't they break up like a month ago?"

"Yeah, they did. But I can't believe that he hasn't tried to contact one of us."

"Why would he call us when he knew that we didn't like him with Gia. He knew that we hated him."

"This is a moral issue, Jessica. The minute he heard about Gia's death, he should've come here and tried to get as much information from us as he could, and especially about when and where her funeral is going to be."

"I agree with you one hundred percent," she acknowledged.

"Damn! I'm gonna miss her so much," I mentioned while wiping my face with the backs of my hands.

"Me too," Jessica added.

Give Me a Chance to Prove It

My classes started back the next day, but in the morning I called my American Politics professor and asked him for a two-day medical leave pass because of my loss, and he gave it to me. I could've asked for an extended pass, but I felt that it was best if I took things day by day. Besides that, I didn't want to chance the likelihood that I would run into Tyler or his flunkies, Eric and Conner. I wasn't a woman who would allow a man to control me, so if I happened to run into them again and they tried to disrespect me in public, I would rip them to shreds, despite the fact that Tyler previously threatened to kill me if I did. I don't play when it comes to people fucking with me and he was gonna find that out sooner than he thought.

With all the bullshit going on, I let my clothes pile up, so I threw everything that was dirty in my clothes basket and headed to the laundry on our floor. Unfortunately for me, the six washers and dryers were all occupied. I went down to the floor below mine and found three washers and two dryers open. Without hesitation I tossed my clothes into two of the empty washing machines, poured one cup of Tide liquid in each, and paid the $2.50 to start the cycles. After the loads started, I exited the room and headed back upstairs. I pressed the elevator button to go back up to my floor but the elevator was occupied, so I took the stairs instead. I figured what harm could it do? Make me build more strength in my legs?

As soon as I reached the door from the stairwell to my floor, I pulled back on the door to open it, but it wouldn't budge. I put strength behind my second pull, and what do you know, the heavy-ass door opened. But not without straining loudly. "Uhhhhh," I belted out. After it was opened far enough, I walked onto my dorm room floor. "That door has a mind of its own," one of the dorm residents commented as she walked toward me. I didn't know her personally, but I knew that she was new on campus and she always took the stairs. "Sometimes it can be easy to open and sometimes it's not."

"Tell me about it," I commented as I walked by her.

As soon as I passed her, I headed to my room. All I could think about was reading more entries from Gia's diary. She had a lot going on in her life before she passed away, and I was sure that I was gonna find out more as I read further.

"Excuse me," I heard a man say. I looked in the direction of the voice. Standing a few feet away from me was a black guy dressed in plain clothes, and before I could utter one word, he beat me to the punch. "Are you Yoshi Lomax?" he asked as he walked toward me. It was a no-brainer that he had just gotten off the elevator.

"Who are you?" I asked him.

He opened his jacket and revealed his police badge. "I'm Detective Fitch, and I'm here to ask you some questions about the rape allegations you filed yesterday," he explained.

Good thing that none of the dorm residents were around,

because he could've leaked all my personal business. "Where would you like to go? My room?" I asked him.

"Sure. Let's go in your room," he agreed, and followed me in.

"You have two roommates?" he asked me after walking into my room and seeing two other beds.

"I only have one roommate now. My other roommate committed suicide. But I thought that maybe one of your colleagues would've mentioned that before you came here," I replied nonchalantly after closing the door behind us.

"Oh yes, I did hear something about that. Sorry for your loss." He offered his condolences. "Is there somewhere I can sit down?" he added.

I pointed to the chair near my bed. Immediately after he sat down, he opened a black leather folder used to carry sensitive and important documents.

"How are you doing today?" he started the conversation off.

"I wish that I knew how to answer that," I replied, and sat down on the edge of my bed.

"Okay, so I see here that you filed a report on an alleged rape at a party that occurred on April fifth by the football player Tyler Egan," he said, reading from a typed document.

"Yes."

"I also see that you didn't get a rape exam performed."

"I told the other cop why I didn't do it," I commented.

"According to the report, you didn't provide the clothing you were wearing at the time of the alleged rape."

"Why do you keep saying 'alleged rape'? That asshole raped me. He put his nasty dick inside of me when I repeatedly told him to stop. He even hit me in my face after I kicked him in his stomach."

"As an officer of the law, I have to use the word *alleged* until the accused is convicted."

"Well, I'm not an officer of the law. Tyler raped me and he's gonna pay for it too."

"Did you ever locate the undergarments you wore on the night of the incident?" the detective asked me, totally ignoring my outburst.

"No. My roommate mistakenly threw it out when she threw out all the other trash we had in the room."

"That's too bad. We're gonna need something to charge Mr. Egan with. Your word alone isn't gonna do it."

"Did you come all the way over here to tell me that?" I raised my voice a little.

"I can understand your frustration, but you've gotta give us something to work with. We have your recorded account of what happened, but we can't take that alone to the DA and ask him to indict Mr. Egan."

"So what's gonna happen now?"

"If you don't have any witnesses that I can talk to who will corroborate your story, then all I can do is talk to Tyler Egan and get his side of the story. After I speak with him, I'm gonna add his account to the report and see where things go from there."

"He's gonna lie and you know it."

"Now don't rush to judgment. I've investigated a lot of rape cases and caught the perpetrator in lies. All it takes is two to three interviews, and if there's deception, it will be revealed."

"Oh please, I won't hold my breath. But I'm telling you this, if you don't get him for what he did to me, then I'm gonna do it myself," I threatened.

"You may not wanna say that," he warned me.

"I can say what I want. Now do your job and arrest that son of a bitch!" I spat.

The detective stood up from the chair and held out his

business card. "Take my card and call me if you have any new information."

"Put it on the desk behind you," I instructed him.

He turned around and dropped his business card on my desk, then he walked over to my dorm room door. "Have a good day," he said, and let himself out of my room. I stood there and watched him leave.

"Fucking jerk-off!" I hissed, and slammed my door.

Annoyed by the way the interview went with that lame-ass cop, I grabbed Gia's diary from my hiding spot and headed back out the room. I figured that since I had some reading material, my time in the laundry would go by fast.

When I arrived back in the laundry room, both of my clothing loads had ended, so I took them out of the washers and tossed them into the dryer. After I paid the $2.50 for a full cycle, it started up and the timer began.

I sat down on one of the three chairs lined up against the wall and dove back into Gia's diary. Once again, she added entries of the dark times that she spent with that idiot-ass nigga she was fucking with. But when I read the name Kristen Chambers, my heart nearly jumped out of my chest.

On August 25, she wrote this entry:

Embarrassed by yet another berating tantrum performed by Scott over the phone while with another girl, I took a walk through the courtyard of the campus alone trying to figure out once and for all how to get up the gumption to leave him and never call him again. I've gotta come to the realization that he does not deserve me. I am too good for him. But then when I get to that point, I think about if I let him go permanently, he'll go off and be with another girl and they'll have a nice and happy life together. I can't allow that to happen. I've put too much time and energy into this relationship. I can't let another woman win. I could feel like a failure.

While I was trying to piece my thoughts together, I see the girl Kristen Chambers talking and giggling with the football player Tyler Egan in front of the frat house. I can't believe how happy she was. He was grabbing her and hugging her. I saw him kiss her a few times. It was so refreshing seeing a man treat a girl the way he was treating her. And that alone spoke volumes to me. So, there is good guys out there in the world that would love and treat a girl right. But what about me? I'm a good girl. I'm nice and I'm smart. So, why I can't have what she's got. Tyler Egan is a popular athlete on campus. Girls would stand in line to have a chance to be with him. But look at him showing one girl that she's special.

I never called Scott back tonight. I wanted to but I didn't. I need to show him that I'm not just gonna let him do what he wants to do and then come back the next day and tell me that the girl he was with was a friend. Or tell me that nothing happened with them. God, will you turn my heart off? Will you take the love I have for Scott away? I'm tired of being in love one day and being hurt the next day. I can't do this alone, God, so please help me.

Pissed off once again by Gia's diary entry, I sat there in a fit of rage. It was sickening. But that wasn't all. The fact that she saw Kristen Chambers the night she went missing was eerie. At that very moment, everything going on between Tyler and me led me to believe that he may have had something to do with Kristen Chambers's disappearance. Now, I didn't have any evidence to support that thought, but from the way he treated me, put his hands on me, I knew that he was capable of doing it. Oh my God! I might be onto something.

Eager to find out if Gia had anything else to say about Kristen Chambers, I scanned every page, looking for her name, but I didn't see it. I even looked back from the beginning and sifted through her entire diary again. But Gia never mentioned her name again. At this point, I felt defeated. Here I was looking for a needle in the haystack but couldn't find it. But then as I looked closely, I realized that several pages of Gia's diary were missing. Someone had torn them out of the book. This made me very suspicious. Were there entries in that diary that pertained to what happened to Kristen Chambers? And if so, then who took them out? And what exactly did Gia say?

Frustrated by this, I sucked my teeth and closed the diary. It was a small leather binder, so it closed with a flap kind of sound. It shocked me, and I startled one of the dorm residents who walked into the laundry room at the very same time.

"Ahhhh, you scared me," the petite white girl said while carrying a sky-blue laundry basket.

"Sorry about that," I apologized. She was another resident I didn't know personally but I'd seen her around on campus. I could tell that she wasn't the talkative type who would spark up a conversation with a complete stranger, because as soon as she started her wash loads, she exited the laundry room without a *Talk to you later* spiel or *Kiss my ass*. She was in and out. That's it.

Despite how pissed off I was that Gia didn't give up more information concerning Kristen Chambers, I thought that I'd be able to sit through the drying cycle of my clothes without cracking Gia's diary back open, but I couldn't. For me, it became a thing that I needed to know how her heart worked.

What made her put up with all the things that Scott took her through? Was she abused as a child? Was she mentally incapable of loving herself? What was it? I thought that the more I learned about who she really was, then I'd know why we lost her.

I skipped more entries in her diary when she talked about Scott, but when she mentioned that she witnessed her father put his hands on her mother and after not doing it for over five years, she went head first in a state of depression. The entry was dated August 30.

I called my mother this evening. I was happy to hear her voice because it had been a while since we talked. We talked about her new diet since finding out that her cholesterol levels were high. Every part of our conversation was going well until my dad walked in the house and asked her where was his dinner? She told him that she took a nap earlier and slept longer than she normally does, but she would get up after she got off the phone with me. But my dad didn't like those plans and instructed her to get off the phone but she protested. She even embarrassed him by telling me that he was drinking again. She said, "Gia, your dad has started drinking again. And for the past week, he hasn't come straight home from work." I could only imagine the hurt and rage building up inside of him after my mother let the cat out the bag because the room became eerily silent. But then without warning I heard one loud clap sound and then I heard a loud thud. I knew then that my dad hit my mother and she fell down on the floor. I heard him tell her that if he ever heard her telling anyone else about what goes on in his house, he would kill her. I felt helpless and wished that I was there to help her but I couldn't so I

*ended the call. It'd been at least seven years since my
dad had put his hands on my mother. As a child I used
to hear him beating her up every night in their
bedroom after he came in the house drunk. So, to re-
flect back on those days of my childhood and at the
same time hearing him treat her like that made my
heart heavy. I instantly started crying and at the same
time shouting through the phone, telling him to stop
before I disconnected the call. My mother didn't
deserve to be treated that way. She was a good woman,
mother and wife. She made so many sacrifices for our
family. So for him to do that to her angered me. I knew
that if my brother was there, he'd beat up my dad
without thinking twice about it.*

*I wished that I could afford to bring her here to
Norfolk, Virginia. I would move out of my dorm and
get an apartment for the both of us. I know that she
would fight me on getting her to move here, but I
wouldn't let up. Her excuse would be that she was the
only person that could take care of my dad. But what
was he doing for her? I swear, sometimes I just want to
take her head off her shoulders and then screw it back
on. Now I know that I am the pot calling the kettle
black, but Scott isn't putting his hands on me. Our
problem is that he cheats on me. That's it. I don't think
that I would tolerate a man cheating on me and beating me up. I would be a fool to. Thank God that my
mother finally had gotten off the floor and got away
from my dad. It took her at least two minutes to do it.
I yelled through the phone for her to pick it up. I even
yelled at my dad and told him that I was going to call
the cops on him if he put his hands on her again. I
heard him telling me to shut up in the background. But
he was saying it as he walked his ass back out of the*

*house. I ended up talking to my mother for at least an-
other hour trying to get her to stop crying. Before we
hung up, I reminded her at least a dozen times of how
beautiful she was and how much my brother and I
loved her. I even reminded her that she went through
years of being abused by my dad when I was a child
and that she shouldn't ever tolerate that kind of abuse
anymore. She promised me that she wouldn't but only
time will tell.*

To read Gia's diary and find out that her mother suffered years of abuse at the hand of her father explained why Gia allowed Scott to treat her the way that he did. And the fact that Gia thought that her situation with Scott was better because Scott didn't put his hands on her. Too bad no one told Gia differently.

Let the Games Begin

Once I had my clean clothes folded neatly in my laundry basket, I hopped on the elevator and headed back to my floor. When I walked into my dorm room, Jessica was changing clothes. She smelled like she had just gotten out of the shower.

"Are you leaving back out?" I asked her as I sat my laundry basket on my bed. I sat down next to it.

"Yes, you're going too," she said.

"Going where?"

"To the mall with me to find a pair of black pants to wear to Gia's wake tomorrow."

"No, I'm not in the mood to go to the mall," I told her.

"Why not?"

"Because I don't feel like it," I replied.

"Are you tired of being in this room all day, every day?"

"Sometimes. But I feel safer staying in here than being out there with all the psychos roaming around on campus. Speaking of which, did Gia ever tell you that her father physically abused her mother for years when she was a child?"

"No, she never mentioned it to me. Why you ask?"

"Because she wrote it in her diary. And now it makes sense why she put up with so much shit from Scott. She was looking for love," I began to explain.

"You got her diary?" Jessica looked at me surprised.

"Yes, and it has some frightening stuff in there. If you knew half of the shit she wrote in there, you would probably cry."

"What kind of stuff did she write?"

"Just about every time Scott mistreated her. The girls that he cheated on her with. Problems that her mother had with her dad and that he was an alcoholic. And check this out, she even mentioned that she saw Kristen Chambers the night she went missing."

Shocked by my admission, she said, "No way!"

"Yes way. And guess where she was?"

"Where?"

"On campus with Tyler Egan. The same motherfucker that raped me."

By this time, Jessica's mouth was wide open. She even sat down on the edge of her bed, giving me her undivided attention. "Oh my God! Do you think that he killed her and hid her body somewhere?"

"I thought that when I first saw her name in Gia's diary, but when I went through the rest of it, Gia never mentioned her name again. I just think that it was a coincidence she saw her."

"Oh my God! But what if that was the case? What if she knew he killed or kidnapped Kristen? Wouldn't that be crazy?"

"Yes, it would," I agreed.

Knock! Knock! Knock! "Open up this fucking door!" the voice on the other side of the door demanded.

Startled, Jessica and I looked at each other as we always

do when we get visitors who haven't warned us beforehand that they are going to stop by. Before Jessica or I could ask the person to announce themselves, the door burst open and there standing at the entryway of our dorm room was Tyler Egan. He looked straight at me. And standing behind him was his frat brother Conner. Conner was his little bitch. Wherever Tyler tell him to go, Conner went.

"You went to the cops and told them that I raped you?" he roared, as if steam were shooting out of both nostrils, and he bolted toward my bed. His eyes were bloodshot red, the veins in his forehead protruding enormously. When he reached me, he grabbed me by my hair and tried to snatch me up on my feet.

"Get off me! Let my hair go!" I screamed loud so that everyone on my floor could hear me and come to my room to see what was going on.

Conner stood at the doorway as the lookout guy. I guess it was their plan to make sure no one came in the room while Tyler did what he came here to do. Thankfully Jessica was there. She hopped off her bed as soon as Tyler grabbed me.

"Get your fucking hands off her," she spat, trying to peel his fingers one by one from my hair. But she was no match for him.

"Let my hair go, you fucking piece of shit. You love putting your hands on women, you fucking coward," I yelled as I began to hit him in the arms and chest with my fists.

"Shut up, you bitch! You fucking whore! You gave me your pussy," he growled while trying to wrap my hair around his hand.

I swear, this shit was hurting like crazy. My scalp was on fire. It felt like with each yank my hair was loosening up and at any given moment that I was gonna end up with patches of my hair missing.

"Jessica, get him off me! He's pulling out my hair," I shouted to the hills.

"Let her fucking hair go, Tyler. Conner, will you please help me!" Jessica belted out with exhaustion. She sounded winded, but she was still in the fight trying to get this idiot off me.

"Come on, Tyler, let's go. Some girls are coming. They're running this way," Conner warned him.

"No, this bitch has to learn that she can't spread lies around about me." He continued to yank my head back and forth. But Conner couldn't stand around and allow the girls to see Tyler attacking me, so he ran into our room, pried Tyler's hands away from my hair with much force, grabbed Tyler in a bear hug, and pulled him away from me.

While Conner was pulling Tyler out of my room, a couple of the dorm residents were peering in at all the commotion caused by Tyler. Sitting there with some of my hair in my hands, I shouted at the top of my voice that he was a rapist. And boy did that infuriate him.

"That motherfucker right there is a rapist. He raped me the other night at his frat party. Stay away from him, because he a woman beater too," I roared. I wanted everyone with ears to hear what I had to say.

"You fucking bitch!" he shouted through clenched teeth, trying to break loose of Conner's grasp. "I'm gonna fucking kill you!" he threatened, still trying to get away from Conner.

Thankfully, Conner was able to pull Tyler out of our room, because I believed that if he hadn't, Tyler would've beat me to a pulp.

After Conner had gotten Tyler as far away as he could, Jessica slammed our door and locked it. Even though Tyler was gone, the aches and pains coming from my scalp hadn't. I was scared to get off the bed to get a look at myself in the mirror and see the damage that Tyler had caused. I was too afraid, especially after seeing the hair I had in my hands.

I started sobbing. "Do you see all this hair he took out of my head?"

"It's not that much," Jessica said. But I knew her, and I knew when she was lying. And this was one of those times.

"Stop, Jessica, don't lie to me," I replied as tears fell from my eyes.

"I'm not lying to you, Yoshi. It's not that much. Here, let me brush it," she insisted as she grabbed her wig brush from her lamp table. She brushed my hair lightly, and by the time she was done, she held out her hand, giving me permission to take my hair from her hand. When I looked at it, it wasn't as much hair as I thought it would be. But I was definitely getting it on the other end, because my entire head was throbbing. I needed some aspirin extremely bad, and I got Jessica to give me a couple from her stash.

I lay down on my bed and waited for the aspirin to kick in, but the effects were taking too long, so I got Jessica to give me two more aspirin. But once again, they weren't working. "Give me a Xanax," I instructed her.

"Are you sure you wanna take one?"

"Of course, I'm sure. Now give it to me," I replied.

Seeing how annoyed I was getting, Jessica grabbed a Xanax from the same bottle she had her aspirin in and handed it to me. I threw it in my mouth so fast. And what do you know, in less than ten minutes later, it was working. And before I knew it, I had fallen asleep.

Fool Me Once

The Xanax I had taken earlier knocked me clean out. When I looked at the clock on my nightstand, I realized that I had been asleep for seven hours. It was 8:11 p.m., and Jessica was nowhere in sight.

I got up from the bed and headed to the bathroom. I literally had to drag myself slowly, trying not to move my head for fear of it throbbing to the point that I would have to take another Xanax.

Once I had used the bathroom, I realized that I was thirsty, so I grabbed two bucks from my purse and headed out of my room. The vending machines were on the first floor of the dorm, so I willed my way onto the elevator and took it all the way to the first-floor lobby. I knew that I was going to be the topic of conversation when I walked by whoever was downstairs, but I could not have cared less. Chicks get beat up by guys every day. But the difference between them and me is that I won't tolerate it. I was gonna report Tyler's ass to the Student Affairs office as soon as I got up in the morning. That asshole was going to get it from all angles. I was talking about rape charges, assault, and threatening bodily harm. And if I could find other ways to put his ass in jail, I would do that too.

I was shocked to see the lobby area somewhat empty. Three girls were sitting down in three areas of the room, and all of them were reading magazines or otherwise busy. And what was weird was that only one of them looked at me. And coincidentally it was Penny. She was reading a textbook so I figured that she was studying.

"Hey, you," she greeted me after looking up from her book.

I waved. But apparently that wasn't enough, because she closed her book and stood up.

Seeing her walk toward me gave me a small level of anxiety because I knew that she was going to ask me a bunch of questions about what happened earlier.

"Give me a moment. Gonna get a soda really quick," I told her so she wouldn't bombard me while I was buying a soda from the vending machine.

I couldn't believe that I stalled her. I actually thought that she was going to follow me and breathe down my neck. For the first time in days, I told someone to do something concerning me and they did it. What a relief.

So while I waited for my Diet Sprite to drop down into the slot, I stood there and wondered about what kind of questions she was going to ask me. I knew that I had to get mentally prepared for her because she was relentless when it came to getting into other people's business. I could only hope that what she was about to ask me wouldn't take me long to answer. I wanted to go back to my dorm room, not hang out down here and become the topic of discussion.

"Oh my God! I heard about what happened earlier. Are you okay?" she started off saying as she approached me. But I didn't just stand there. I made her walk with me to the elevator while I held my cold can of Diet Sprite.

"What did you hear?" I asked her. I wasn't giving away any information. I wanted to know what she knew or heard.

"I heard that that football player Tyler attacked you and that he pulled clumps of hair from your head."

"Who told you that?" I continued to question her all while walking toward the elevator. I pressed the button immediately after I got within arm's reach.

"The girls that live on your floor. They said that you accused him of raping you at the party he had a week ago and told the cops."

"Yes, I did," I answered her, and then the elevator door opened. I stepped inside of it and she followed me.

"I'm sorry to hear that," she said as the door closed.

"Don't be sorry, because he will pay for it. Just like he did when he attacked me earlier."

"So tell me if I'm wrong, did he attack you the other day for the same thing?"

"Yes, he did."

"I knew I heard you say that he raped you. That piece of shit. Do you know how many girls worship him?"

"I have an idea."

"I hope you bury his ass."

"I'm trying to. But I keep running into road blocks."

"What kind of road blocks?" she pressed me at the same time that the elevator door opened. I stepped off, and once again she followed me.

"I went to the precinct, reported him to the cops. They took my statement and sent me on my merry way."

"What do you mean by that?"

"The cop asked me if I had the results from my rape exam, and I told him that I didn't go to the hospital after he raped me but that I ran back to my dorm and took a shower because I wanted to get his smell off me."

"Was this the same night I saw you from my dorm room?"

"Yes, it was that exact night."

"Oh my, I'm so sorry that I didn't come and help you. When I saw you, I knew something was wrong with you. But when I asked you about it the very next day, you didn't mention it."

"That was because I wasn't in the mind frame to talk about it. I was shocked that it happened to me," I explained as she and I walked down the hall toward my room.

"What about the clothes you were wearing that night? Did you take those with you when you filed the rape report?"

"No, because after I took them off, I threw them in a plastic bag and Jessica made a mistake and threw them in the trash."

"Oh no. So what are you going to do now?"

"I don't know. But I'll tell you this, I am not letting this matter go. He is going to pay for what he did to me. Not only did that bastard rape me, he assaulted me while he raped me, he almost choked my lights out when you saw him holding me up in the air, and then he came to my room and put his hands on me again."

"If you need me to be a witness and say that I saw you running back to the dorm on the night he raped you, I will."

"That's not enough. They need either the rape kit results or my clothes. And even that may not do anything to help me, because the cop I spoke to today told me that I needed a witness or it would be a thing where it would be my word against his."

Penny shook her head in dismay. "I am truly sorry that you're going through this. I know that this has gotta be mentally challenging, especially with the death of your roommate."

"Yeah, it's been rough," I said while opening the door to my room.

"Is that where she slept?" Penny asked me as she followed me into the room.

"Yes, and every time I look over there I sink deeper into depression."

"I'm sure you do," she said as she sat down on the chair near Gia's bed.

"When is her funeral?"

"In two days. Her wake is tomorrow."

"Going?"

"Yes, I'm going to the wake. But not her funeral."

"Why not?"

"Because her parents blame me for her suicide. They think that I introduced her to prescription drugs."

"Really?"

"Yes, and they're all wrong."

"I'm sorry you're going through that."

"Me too. I just wish that they'd see that I'm telling the truth."

"So where did she get the drugs from?"

"From Rita," I said without even realizing I said it. Penny looked at me in shock.

"Rita who?" She pressed the issue. But I knew that I had said enough. I wasn't about to throw Rita under the bus. She comes from a dangerous family, so I was closing my mouth about her right then and there.

"I'm not sure of her last name," I lied.

"Does she live here on campus? Or go to school here?" she wanted to know.

"I don't think so."

"That's too bad because if you knew, then you could prove your case to Gia's parents that you had nothing to do with her death," Penny continued.

What she said made sense, but I wasn't getting myself involved with who and where Gia got the prescription drugs from. Besides, I don't know this chick here for real. For all I know, she could be a fucking cop, and as of now I don't like cops. They are lazy and they do not protect and serve.

I chatted with Penny for a few more minutes and then I acted like I needed to be alone so that I could get some school work done. Thankfully, she obliged and left as soon as I mentioned it. The truth of the matter was, it was something that rubbed me the wrong way with her. She always seemed to be around when something bad happened. I hoped I was wrong. But then again, I knew I could be right.

What Just Happened?

After Penny left my room, I dug in my laundry basket to get Gia's diary so that I could dig further into her mind to get more acquainted with who she was, but the diary wasn't there. I didn't get a chance to put my clothes away earlier because of the incident with Tyler, so it should have still been there. To make sure that I didn't overlook it, I dumped all of my folded clothes onto my bed and sifted through every garment I had washed. Unfortunately, I still couldn't locate it. "Where the fuck is it?" I whispered to myself.

I started retracing my steps, and that led me to go back down to the laundry room where I was washing my clothes earlier. I took the staircase down to the floor beneath mine because that's what I did to get to the laundry room the first time. As I walked down the hallway, I searched the floor all the way until I reached the laundry room, but it was nowhere in sight.

To continue retracing my steps, I got back on the elevator and took it back up to my floor. When the elevator door opened, I stepped off and walked back in the direction of my dorm room, all while searching the floor with my eyes to see if I had mistakenly dropped it. Once again, it was nowhere in sight.

Instantly panic-stricken, I headed back into my room and started searching underneath all the beds and chairs, in the lockers and closets, but I couldn't find Gia's diary. "Where the hell are you?" I said aloud, hoping that it would jog my memory. But of course, it didn't.

Puzzled and perplexed by this, I came to the conclusion that Gia's diary wasn't in this room and the only person who could've taken it was Jessica. And then the question was, Why? Why would you take something that didn't belong to you? What was her purpose? I guessed that the only way I would get the answer was to ask her when I saw her.

While I waited for Jessica to call our dorm room or show up in person, I got a call from Maria.

"Hello?"

"Don't hello me, Yoshi. Why didn't you call me earlier and tell me that that piece of shit Tyler put his freaking hands on you? And please tell me that he's in jail for assaulting you," she spat. The volume of her voice went up a couple of notches.

"Who told you?" I wanted to know. I figured that if she knew what happened to me, then the campus security should know it as well.

"My roommate Abby told me. She has a study partner that lives in your dorm. But never mind all that, tell me what happened," she said.

"I went to the precinct yesterday and filed a report against Tyler for raping me, and when the detective stopped by his dorm and told him what I did, he stormed over to my dorm and started attacking me."

"Are you freaking kidding me?" Maria sounded appalled.

"No, I'm serious. And I'm gonna make sure that he gets arrested on campus in front of everyone. He needs to know that he just can't put his hands on people and not reap the consequences."

"I second that. So when are you going to press charges against him?"

"I'm going in the morning."

"Why tomorrow morning?"

"Because Jessica was here. She witnessed the whole thing. Not only that, I think she's gonna file charges of assault too."

"Where is she now?"

"She had to run an errand."

"Would you like me to go with you?"

"Of course I would love that. I need as much support as I can possibly get."

"Do you have any cuts and bruises on you?"

"I have a couple of scratches around my face. But I'm feeling the most pain in the scalp area of my head. He took a lot of my hair out too."

"I wish that I was there when he put his hands on you. I swear, by the time I was finished with his ass, he would've walked out of your dorm room blind."

"I wish you were here too."

"He should be kicked out of school because of that. Have you contacted Student Affairs?"

"No, but I will in the morning."

"Remember he's a poster boy for the university. His coaches and the student body will make it hard for you to take him down, so be prepared for some backlash."

"I'm ready for it."

"I hope you are."

I chilled in my room and watched the clock go from 9:00, to 10:30, then to 11:23, and finally the time turned to 12:51. Between those times, I called all her friends in the other dorms, but they said that they hadn't seen her since earlier.

"Where the hell are you?" I said, pacing the floor. It

seemed like I was running out of floor space in my dorm room, so I decided to go down to the lobby to see if Jessica was down there running her mouth to one of the other residents. If she wasn't there, then she had to be sleeping out with one of her many boyfriends. She wasn't exclusive, so she could be with anyone.

The time that it took me to get from my dorm room to the lobby of the dorm was less than forty-five seconds flat. But it was all in vain because the lobby was completely empty, so I went outside. Standing at the front door of the dorm, I could look around the whole courtyard and see that it was as empty as the lobby, so there was no need for me to leave the building. I turned around and went back upstairs to my dorm room and waited for Jessica there.

Someone Will Pay for This

After tossing and turning all night, I got out of bed at 7:52 a.m., and when I looked at Jessica's bed, she was not in it. So, I called all the dorm rooms of her friends and every one of them still said that they hadn't seen her.

"Jessica, where the hell are you?" I spat after I slammed the cordless phone down on the desk.

Immediately after I threw the phone down, it started ringing. I scrambled to the desk and snatched it up.

"Hello," I said.

"What time will you be ready to take the trip to the police station?" When I heard Maria's voice, I knew that it was a false alarm.

"I'm waiting on Jessica. As soon as she gets here, I'll be ready to leave."

"How are you feeling this morning? Does your head feel any better?"

"Just a little. I'm gonna take a couple more aspirin. Hopefully, it works."

"I want you to take it easy. Two aspirins and that's it."

"I know."

"Call me when you're ready."

"I will."

Seconds after I ended the call with Maria, I started thinking what if something happened to Jessica?

Going along with my gut feeling, I decided to take the elevator down to the first-floor lobby again. A lot of the dorm residents hang out down there and drink coffee and hot chocolate before they head to class. I thought since Jessica does this from time to time, then she could be down there in the small crowd.

On my way to the elevator, I said good morning to everyone I passed. I even asked a couple of them if they'd seen Jessica this morning. Every one of them said that either they hadn't seen her since the afternoon before or they hadn't seen her at all.

Downstairs in the lobby I got the same answers as the ones I got from the dorm residents on my floor. This scared me. So I stepped out of the dorm and sat down on one of the metal benches outside. There I peered around the courtyard as far as I could see, but all I saw were students and a handful of faculty staff members.

"What's good, Yoshi. You a'ight?" I heard a voice say from behind me. I looked over my left shoulder and realized that it was Rita making her early morning runs. One thing about this chick, she knew how to hustle and peddle everyone's prescription fix on campus.

"Yes, I'm good. Why you ask?"

"I heard about that shit that happened between you and that dude Tyler," she replied as she worked her way from behind me to the side of me and then was standing before me.

"Tell me who hasn't heard it?"

Rita chuckled. "I wouldn't tolerate a dude hitting on me. I

would have him crushed to smithereens if he did that shit to me."

"Oh, don't worry, his time is coming sooner than anyone knows," I stated, and then I changed the subject. "Have you seen my roommate, Jessica?"

"Not since yesterday. Why?"

"Because that's the last time I saw her too."

"Have you checked the frat house? I saw her standing outside talking to Conner. Oh yeah, I forgot you can't go there," she mentioned as she realized that I had the beef with Tyler.

"Did you see her go inside?" I pressed Rita.

"No. Just standing outside," Rita continued. "Hit me up if you need anything," she said as she walked away.

I sat there on the bench, looking puzzled, trying to figure out whether Jessica talked to Conner before she and I had our conversation or after. If it was after, then she definitely had some explaining to do.

After sitting there on the bench for what seemed like an hour, I went back inside the dorm and used the phone in the lobby and dialed Jessica's best friend Lisa's dorm room phone number. She answered on the second ring.

"Hello," she said.

"Hey, Lisa, this is Yoshi, I'm calling you back to see if you talked to Jessica yet?"

"Nope. Not since yesterday. And now I'm beginning to get worried," she replied.

"Think Chelsea talked to her yet?" I wanted to know.

"I haven't spoken to Chelsea since last night. So I wouldn't know," Lisa replied.

"Okay, well, I'm gonna call her now on three-way. Hold on," I told Lisa, and then I clicked over to a new phone line. When the other line started ringing, I conferenced Lisa back in. "Lisa, are you on the line?" I asked her simultaneously as the other call rang.

"Yes, I'm here."

"Hello?" I heard Chelsea after the fourth ring.

"Hey, Chelsea, it's me, Yoshi, and I've got Lisa on three-way."

"Hey, Chelsea," Lisa said.

"Hi, Lisa, what's going on?" Chelsea replied.

"We still haven't talked to Jessica, so we were wondering had you seen or talked to her?" I asked.

"No, I still haven't heard from her," Chelsea announced. "Maybe she's with Conner. He's all she talks about."

"Yeah, you're right. I asked her yesterday why would she even be speaking to him after she saw Tyler beat you up," Lisa agreed.

"What did she say?" I wanted to know.

"She said that I was overexaggerating because it's not like Conner hit you himself. And that Conner was the one that was trying to break up the fight," Lisa explained.

"But that's not the point. He was with Tyler. And speaking of which, Lisa, remember when you dropped me off after we left the hospital?"

"Yeah."

"While I was walking back to my dorm, Tyler and Conner started talking shit to me. Tyler was like, Yoshi, thanks for showing me a good time. And then Conner was like, Oh yeah, Yoshi, I heard that you were a good kisser. And then there was a third guy but he didn't say anything. All he did was laugh like he was at a comedy club."

"Fucking jerk-offs!" Chelsea yelled.

"Yeah, that's fucked up," Lisa agreed.

"Hey, you guys, does she have any classes this morning?" I asked them both.

"I don't think she does." Lisa answered first.

"I don't think she does either," Chelsea replied.

"Tell you what, you guys, call the frat house for me. And if she's there, let her know that I am looking for her," I told them both.

"Sure," Lisa said.

"Will do," Chelsea agreed.

Once I cleared the line of Chelsea and Lisa, I went up to my room and hopped in the shower, then got dressed. I even sat around the room waiting for Jessica to call me back. She knew we had a laundry list of shit we agreed to do today. First off, we needed to file charges on Tyler for assaulting me yesterday. And we had to go to Gia's wake, since I would not be able to go to the funeral. Everything was weighing heavily on my heart so I had to get those things done.

I waited around for another hour hoping that Jessica would walk through the door or call me back, but none of those things happened. So I called Maria and had her take me to the police station to file assault charges on Tyler.

After I arrived at the precinct I learned that when you file assault charges, it goes before a magistrate, not the cops. So I sat down with a female magistrate, and filed assault charges on Tyler. It felt so good filing those charges. I even filed a restraining order against Tyler too. He couldn't come within 100 feet of me. Having this legal document in my hand made me feel liberated. And what do you know, I didn't have to have Jessica there to be my witness. I was told that she would have to show up to court, but as of right now, no. I was good and I was happy.

When I left the magistrate's office, I headed back to the dorm, and as soon as I walked into my room and saw that Jessica hadn't made it back, I picked up the phone and called Maria.

"Girl, I'm about to lose my mind."

"Why?"

"Because Jessica still hasn't come back."

"Where do you think she could be?" Maria asked me.

"Maria, I wish I had the answer. I've been looking for her since yesterday."

"Has she ever done this before?"

"No. I don't think she has. I mean, if she has, I don't remember her doing it."

"What are her friends saying?"

"They said the same thing as me. The last time they saw her was yesterday and she was standing in front of the frat house."

"Well, let's just hope that she comes back soon."

"I second that."

It seemed like immediately after I hung up the phone from Maria, I got yet another call. I knew it had to be Jessica finally calling me back.

"Jessica, please tell me it's you!"

"Hi, Yoshi, this is Dean Paige. I need you to come to my office at once."

"Okay, but is there something wrong?" I wondered aloud.

"We'll talk about that when you get here. See you soon," she said, and then she disconnected our call.

It took me approximately one and a half minutes to get to Dean Paige's office door from the time I walked into the administrative building. I knocked on her door as soon as I approached it. When it opened, Mr. Donovan, the director of Student Affairs, stood there before me. He smiled and greeted me by shaking my hand.

"How are you?" he said.

"Not so good, but I will be soon," I replied.

Dean Paige was sitting behind her desk, but she stood up and leaned over her desk to shake my hand as well. "Have a seat," she instructed me after she let go of my hand.

I sat down in a chair next to Mr. Donovan. Mr. Donovan was a tall, slim guy with neatly moussed hair and the sharp, distinguished features of a hedge fund executive. He looked like he couldn't be a day over the age of thirty.

"Mr. Donovan and I asked you to come here because of an unfortunate event that happened yesterday between you and Mr. Egan."

"Yes, and we're optimistic that we can solve things between you two before it gets out of hand," Mr. Donovan chimed in.

I sat there looking at both of these fools, wondering where were they going with this conversation. I wasn't liking the vibes I was feeling, but they had my undivided attention.

"So, Mr. Egan says that you attended a party at the frat house. When you arrived, you were given a drink and from there, you and he retreated to a couch in the corner away from the crowd that was there. He said that everything was going well. You and he talked and got to know each other. He then said that you were so smitten with him that you kissed him—"

"That's a lie. He kissed me," I interjected.

"Let me finish and then I'll give you the opportunity to talk," Dean Paige said. "So, like I was saying, you kissed each other, you asked him if you two could go somewhere in the house that was quieter—"

"That's a lie! I didn't say that," I snapped. This version of the story was about to make me flip Dean Paige's desk over.

"She is going to let you give your side of the story, so stop interrupting," Mr. Donovan chimed in.

"Do you know how hard it is to sit here and listen to this mess? There's nothing true about this story," I argued.

"I told you that if you let me finish, you will have your chance to tell your side of the story," Dean Paige added.

I sucked my teeth and sighed heavily. "Okay, go ahead," I replied.

"Like I was saying, after Mr. Egan obliged you, you and he

went to his room and that's when you seduced him. He said that you two had consensual sex. You tried to contact him the next day to see where you two could take the relationship, and that's when he told you that you and he had a one-night stand. To get back at him, you began to spread rumors that he raped you."

"No disrespect to you, Dean Paige, but he's a damn liar. I didn't seduce him. He started kissing me. And it was his idea to go to his room. When we got in there, I sat down on his bed because he said that all we were going to do was talk. But that didn't happen. Instead, he started kissing me. I didn't mind the kissing, but when he began to undress himself, I told him flat out that I wasn't trying to have sex with him."

"What did he say?" Mr. Donovan asked.

"He started ranting about how I was being a big tease and that he wasn't gonna let me out of his room unless I had sex with him. I told him no and proceeded to get off his bed, but he pushed me back and climbed on top of me. After he climbed on top of me, he snatched off my pants. I started kicking and telling him to stop but he wouldn't listen, so I kicked him really hard in his stomach, and when I did that, he smacked me really hard in my face two times and told me if I did it again, he was going to kill me. So I stopped fighting him."

"You stopped fighting him and did what?" Dean Paige asked.

"I let him rape me," I told her.

"You mean you let him have sex with you? Because you don't let someone rape you." Mr. Donovan corrected me.

"Are you kidding me right now? I had no other choice but to let that rapist rape me. He hit me really hard. And I couldn't match his strength. He's a freaking athlete," I pointed out. These two motherfuckers were about to get all the F-bombs I could muster up.

"I saw you the day after this alleged incident. So why didn't you tell me then?" Dean Paige asked me.

"Because I was uncertain whether I was going to press charges against him."

"Why were you uncertain?" Mr. Donovan chimed back in.

"Look, it's difficult to explain."

"Ms. Lomax, either he raped you or he didn't. Now, which one was it?" Dean Paige pressed me.

"Tyler Egan raped me. And the only reason why I didn't say anything before was because I didn't go straight to the emergency room to get a rape kit exam right after it happened. And because I wanted to get proper counsel from my parents."

"But then you went forward and filed rape charges against Mr. Egan," Mr. Donovan said aloud, directing the statement at me.

"Yes, I did."

"Looks like you're gonna have to rescind your statement," Dean Paige stated. But it sounded more like a demand.

"Rescind my statement for what? He raped me and you're acting like I'm falsely accusing him of doing so." I raised my voice. "Just like yesterday. Did you know that he stormed into my dorm room and almost beat me to death? If it weren't for my roommate, Jessica, he could've seriously hurt me or, worse, killed me. As a matter of fact, ask Jessica Vonn. She was with me at the party when the rape happened, and she was in our room when Tyler attacked me."

"We've already spoken with her, and she gave us the same story Tyler did. In fact, his fraternity brother Conner gave the same exact story as Jessica," Dean Paige informed me.

"When did she do that?" I didn't believe her for one second that Jessica turned on me like that.

"We have a recording of her giving me that statement," Dean Paige insisted.

"Where is the recording?" I challenged her.

She pulled out a pocket-size handheld voice recorder. She fumbled with the control buttons while I sat there and watched her. A couple seconds later, she powered on the recorder by pressing the play button.

The only voices on the recording were Dean Paige and Jessica.

"What is your name?"

"Jessica Vonn."

"Are you a student here at Old Dominion University?"

"Yes, I am," she replied. She sounded robotic.

"How long have you attended this university?" Dean Paige continued.

"Three years."

"Are you roommates with Yoshi Lomax?"

"Yes."

"Did you attend a party hosted by frat brothers on this campus the other night?"

"Yes, ma'am."

"Did you attend this party alone?"

"No."

"Who attended this party with you?" she wanted to know.

"My roommate Yoshi Lomax."

"At this party, were she and Tyler Egan entertaining each other?"

"Yes."

"At this party, did you witness Yoshi Lomax kiss Tyler Egan?"

"Yes."

"Who pursued who?" Dean Paige pressed Jessica.

"Yoshi pursued Tyler," Jessica replied, sounding more robotic the longer she talked.

"That's a freaking lie. And why does she sound like that?

She sounds like she's high," I roared. I couldn't believe what I was hearing.

Dean Paige stopped the recorder and gave me a stern look. "Yoshi, I know you're upset because of Jessica's statement, but she's your roommate so what would she gain by lying?"

"She sounds like she was high and coached to say what she said," I protested.

"She didn't sound like she was under the influence to me. It sounded like she was giving her version of what happened the night of the party. And now I want you to give me your side of what happened. That way I can make the right call."

"Dean Paige, that's not how my roommate talks. She's slurring her words a little bit. And that mess she told you is false. None of what she said happened that way."

"Want me to replay the audio?" she asked. She wasn't hearing anything I had to say. All she wanted to do was play that dumb-ass tape that she got Jessica to lie on. Something wasn't right with the whole setup.

"Do I have a choice?" I replied in a smug manner.

"Yes, you do."

"But she's lying. I know Jessica, and I can tell when she's lying. And on this recorder, that's exactly what she's doing."

"I don't doubt that you know her, but she seemed pretty sincere to me."

"Can I leave now?"

"Not until we resolve this issue. Now sit back and listen," she demanded, and then she pressed the play button.

"When Tyler and Yoshi kissed, did she look like she enjoyed it?" Dean Paige continued questioning Jessica in the audio interview.

"Yes, she did," Jessica answered.

"That's only because he was acting like a freaking gentleman," I interjected as the audio played.

"Please, Yoshi, stop interrupting while we listen to this,"

Dean Paige said. I could tell that she was losing her patience with me. But in my mind, I couldn't care less. This was a bogus-ass audio statement from Jessica. They tipped the scale on this one.

Instead of commenting, I sucked my teeth and sat back in the chair.

"So you mentioned that you and Yoshi Lomax have been roommates for three years, correct?"

"Correct."

"You've witnessed firsthand the type of men she has dated, correct?"

"Correct."

"You've also seen the number of guys she's been intimate with, correct?"

"Correct."

"Can you give me a ballpark figure of the men you've seen in and out of her life?"

Jessica paused like she was thinking and then said, "In the past three years, I can say that I've seen her with a little over twenty guys."

"That is a lie!" I roared after jumping up on my feet.

"Sit down, Ms. Lomax," Mr. Donovan ordered me.

I ignored his direct order. "That's not true. I've only dated like five guys since I've been here. That's a lie. Someone told her to say that," I protested.

"Sit down, Yoshi," Dean Paige chimed in. Her voice and facial expression were intimidating.

I sat back down in my chair. "Dean Paige, this is not Jessica. Someone is coaching her to say those things," I pointed out.

"Ms. Lomax, when this audio interview was recorded yesterday, there were only three people in the room. Jessica Vonn, me, and a lie detection specialist who teaches sound and videography in the Film Department of this school. So you see, no one coached her. This recording was completely organic," Dean Paige replied.

"Dean Paige, I know my roommate like the back of my hand, so I know when she's lying or afraid of something. And this is one of those times. She knows that I've never been with that many guys. As a matter of fact, she's asked me on several occasions why don't I go out more? She calls me a square, for heaven's sake."

"Since you won't allow me to play the entire recording, I'm forced to tell you that before it ended, Jessica said that she didn't believe that you were raped. In fact, she said that if you had been raped, you would've been more broken up about it and you would've gone to the hospital," Dean Paige explained.

"That's straight-up bullshit!" I shouted and jumped back up on my feet. Mr. Donovan stood up alongside me. "And where is Jessica anyway? She didn't come back to the dorm last night, and I've been trying to find her with no luck," I continued.

"Sit down, Ms. Lomax!" Dean Paige stood up and slammed her fist down on her desk.

"You know what? I don't have to stand here and listen to this mess," I said, and then I turned around and stormed out of Dean Paige's office.

I thought that Mr. Donovan was going to follow me, but he didn't. He stayed back in Dean Paige's office, talking about me of course. It wouldn't have surprised me if I was written up and put on probation. The actions I displayed are usually dealt with swiftly, so I knew I would be hearing from him before the day was over.

While I was walking out of the administrative building, I saw Chelsea and Lisa walking like they were headed to the student parking area of the campus. I yelled both of their names to get their attention. Lisa heard me first and waved at me.

"Hold up," I yelled, and sprinted over to where they were standing.

Out of breath, I finally caught up to them. They both smiled at me.

"You all right?" Lisa said in a joking manner.

"No, not really. Just left Dean Paige's office," I told them both.

"What happened?" Lisa asked.

"She and Mr. Donovan from Student Affairs had me in her office asking me questions about what happened between Tyler and me."

"What did you say?" Chelsea chimed in.

"I told them the truth. But they don't believe that he raped me."

"No way. Really?!" Lisa said.

"But that's not it. Dean Paige pulled out an audio recording of Jessica saying that she didn't think that Tyler raped me. And in that same recording, she also said that I've been with twenty different guys."

"Nooooo," Chelsea commented.

"Wait, so what kind of recording is it?" Lisa wanted to know.

"When Dean Paige found out what happened between Tyler and me, she summoned Jessica to her office and recorded her as she asked Jessica questions."

"Can she do that? Is that legal?" Lisa added.

"I don't know. But this was recorded yesterday, and Jessica sounded like she was drugged up," I stated.

"So, wait, what time of day was this recorded?" Chelsea asked.

"I don't know. I forgot to ask," I replied.

"Well then, that's what we gotta do," Lisa chimed in. "So what did Mr. Donovan say?"

"He was basically helping Dean Paige tag team me. I honestly felt like I was being bullied into recanting my story about what happened at the frat house. And to have statements from Jessica and other students saying that I was kissing Tyler downstairs in front of everyone like I was enjoying myself. And that they didn't believe that I was raped. And do you know that Tyler said that the only reason why I'm pursuing him legally is because I wanted a relationship with him but he in turn said that I was a one-night stand for him? Can you believe that shit? I swear, after I heard that, I had to get out of that office."

"That's messed up," Chelsea commented.

"Did you know that Tyler's dad is a huge donor to this university? So Dean Paige is going to do everything within her power to discredit anything you say about Tyler," Lisa said.

Taken aback by this revelation, I stood there with my mouth wide open as the thoughts in my head started spinning. "Is that why that bitch is trying to discredit me? Fucking backstabber! She doesn't care about women's rights, all she wants are the donations that come through here," I spat. I was freaking livid with this new finding.

"We gotta find Jessica and find out what really went on in Dean Paige's office when she was being recorded," Lisa insisted.

"Yeah, we do. Because this is not her. Something is definitely wrong," I pointed out.

"Don't worry. She's fine. Knowing her, she's probably with one of her new flings if she's not with Conner," Chelsea suggested.

"I hope you're right," I said. "So what are you two getting ready to do now? You know Gia's wake is today?" I continued.

"Yes, as a matter of fact, we were on our way there," Chelsea announced.

"Can I get a ride with you guys? Jessica and I were supposed to go together, but since she's not around, I gotta find another way."

"Sure," Chelsea replied.

"Of course you can," Lisa agreed.

"Thank you, guys."

"No problem. Let's get out of here," Chelsea insisted, and then we walked off together.

Back to the Basics

On the way to the wake, I also thought about the mindset Jessica was in during that audio interview. She was drugged. I know that 100 percent. I won't say that Dean Paige or the Film Department professor drugged her themselves, but I will say that they knew something was off with her too. What was really tugging at me was finding out that Tyler's dad is a huge financial donor to the university, which is why Dean Paige was trying to discredit me. If Tyler was arrested for my rape and for assault, this school would lose a lot of money. Not to mention that ODU would gain a bad reputation. But who cares about this freaking school? I was raped and attacked on three different occasions and Tyler would be dealt with accordingly. I can promise you that.

As Lisa pulled up to the funeral home, I immediately scanned the parking lot to see if I recognized any of the cars belonging to Jessica or Gia's family. I didn't see any. After we exited the car, I took in a deep breath and exhaled.

Knowing that this would be my first time seeing Gia, anxiety began to seep down into the pit of my stomach.

Lisa and Chelsea walked ahead of me. I even said a quiet prayer, asking God to give me the strength to cope with what I was about to see.

"Sign your name in this book," a black woman instructed us after we entered the funeral home. This was proper protocol when you're viewing a body, so one by one, Chelsea, Lisa, and I signed the book.

Afterward, the woman led us into the area where Gia's body was lying. I could see the casket from where I was standing, which was at the entryway of the room. Seeing that, I felt like a blow hit my chest. I almost stopped and turned around to go in the opposite direction, but when I saw how Lisa and Chelsea continued to move forward, I moved forward with them.

The moment we came face-to-face with Gia, I instantly started sobbing. Lisa started crying too, but Chelsea just stood there and watched her. She even touched Gia's hand.

"Her hand kind of feels hard," she said.

"I can't believe she's gone." Lisa sobbed as she looked at Gia from head to toe.

"I can't either," I chimed in.

When people say that your loved ones don't look the same after they die, they are telling the truth. Gia looked as if she had on a mask with painted makeup. Her body looked as if it was filled to capacity with embalming fluid. In my eyes, this was not Gia. This was not my roommate lying in this casket. Gia was young, vibrant, and beautiful. Not like this.

"Gia, I am so sorry that I wasn't there for you when this happened. I miss and love you so much." I was finally able to say it to her.

Lisa said everything from how she's going to miss washing clothes together, having study sessions together, getting their hair done together, going shopping together. Chelsea didn't harp on what she and Gia did together, but Lisa and I knew what Gia meant to her and the many things that they did together. Gia was special in every sense of the word. It didn't matter to us that she made a lot of bad judgment calls. What mattered to us was that we loved each other unconditionally.

We stuck around for about forty-five minutes hoping that Jessica would show up, but she didn't. Who did show up to the funeral home was Gia's family. They walked up behind Lisa, Chelsea, and me while we were sitting in the second row of seats facing Gia's casket.

"What are you doing here?" I heard a woman's voice say. And immediately I knew that it was Gia's mother looming over my shoulder. I turned around slowly and followed Mr. and Mrs. Santos with my eyes as they traveled past me and then ultimately stood before me. No one else was with them.

Instead of answering her, I stood up from my seat and walked in the opposite direction of her and her husband.

"Wait a minute, you don't get to come here after I told you to stay away and then leave while I'm talking to you," Mrs. Santos chastised me.

But I ignored her and continued to walk away.

"You're not leaving until you answer my question," she shouted, and then I heard footsteps running toward me.

"Hold up. Wait a minute," I heard Lisa say, and then I heard more movement, so I turned around and saw that Mrs. Santos was running in my direction while her husband followed her. I assumed that when Lisa and Chelsea saw the Santoses running behind me, they figured that I'd need some help if the Santoses attacked me.

As soon as the Santoses got near me, Mrs. Santos grabbed me by my arm and unleashed her wrath with how she felt about me while Lisa and Chelsea stood within a couple of feet of me.

"I told you to stay away from my daughter, and yet you defy my order. You are a selfish little bitch! You fed my daughter all those damn drugs and now you show your face on the day before I lay her to rest. You are a Godless person, and everything you do or touch from this point on will crumble."

I snatched my arm away from her. "Did you just curse me? Did you just put a hex on me?" I snapped. This lady just put bad juju on me and now I'd have to live with it. She was gonna have to take that back.

"In my country we call it witchcraft," she corrected me. Her voice sounded demonic.

"Take it back!" I demanded as I got in her face.

Without warning Mrs. Santos hocked and spit in my face. The warm saliva felt wet and gross as it slid down my face. I saw red and instantly hauled off and smacked Mrs. Santos in her face. The blow from my hand sent Mrs. Santos flying back into Mr. Santos's arms. He caught her right before she fell to the floor. Lisa and Chelsea stood there in complete shock as I wiped the spit from my face with the sleeve of my jacket.

"What the hell is wrong with you? You can't spit in people's faces like that, especially mine!" I shouted in anger.

After Mr. Santos saved Mrs. Santos from falling down on the floor, he tried to lunge at me, but Lisa and Chelsea got between us by blocking him.

"No, we can't let you do that," Lisa said to Mr. Santos.

"Move the fuck out my way before I thrash you." Mr. Santos threatened both Lisa and Chelsea.

"Get out of his way! That bitch assaulted me and he's gonna make her pay," Mrs. Santos yelled at them from the sideline.

"What is going on in here?" an official from the funeral home asked after he entered the room.

"She hit my wife and I'm gonna make her pay for it," Mr. Santos yelled.

"So you wanna put your hands on me like you do your wife? Yeah, you fucking coward! I read Gia's diary," I ranted.

"What are you talking about?" he responded, looking guilty.

"You guys are gonna have to take this nonsense some-where else. This is a respectable place of business."

"You know what I am talking about." I ignored the fu-neral home employee. "In Gia's diary, she said that you beat her mother as a child almost every night you came home drunk and then you got some help and stopped. But then just recently you started putting your fucking hands on her again. Gia said that in order to deal with you guys, she had to get high because she didn't want to accept the fact that she came from a fucked-up family. So do yourself a favor and keep your hands to yourself before I have your ass sleeping under-neath a bed in a jail cell," I added.

"You don't know what you're talking about. My hus-band has never put his hands on me." Mrs. Santos de-fended him.

"Oh, shut up and stop lying!" I interjected. "Gia started taking drugs because of you. Not me. So get your facts straight. Gia loved me and I loved her, and that's all that mat-ters," I said, and then I turned around and left everyone standing in the home.

I headed outside to Lisa's car, and a minute or so later, Lisa and Chelsea joined me. Their eyes grew as they approached me. Lisa spoke first.

"Wow! That was intense."

"Yes, it was. So Gia's dad used to fight on her mom?" Chelsea asked me.

"That's what Gia put in her diary," I told them.

"That's sad," Lisa added.

"Yeah, it is. I mean, who would've ever known that Gia had to put up with knowing that? I honestly don't think that I could've dealt with something like that," Chelsea commented.

"I don't think that I could've done it either. My mama? Oh hell no!" Lisa chimed back in.

"Can you guys get me out of here?" I asked. I was burnt out with this whole situation dealing with Gia and her parents. I'd been innocent the whole time and they still didn't recognize it, so I said to hell with them both.

In the car, Lisa started grilling me about the content that Gia put in her diary. I really wasn't in the mood to disclose that information to them, but then I realized that they were Gia's best friends and that it was only fair that I give them some insight about the problems that Gia was going through before she committed suicide.

"What else did she say in her diary?" Lisa wanted to know as she maneuvered her way in and out of traffic.

"Yeah, did she say anything about her dumb-ass ex-boyfriend Scott?" Chelsea asked from the front passenger seat.

"Scott's name was almost on every page in her diary. She wrote about all the girls he cheated on her with. The times when he put his hands on her. She wrote about how lonely she was. Oh, and she even wrote about seeing that girl Kristen Chambers the night she went missing."

"Are you kidding me? She said that?" Chelsea commented as she turned around in the seat to face me.

"Yep," I replied.

"What exactly did she say?" Lisa asked.

"She didn't say much, but she saw Kristen talking to Tyler outside the frat house."

"No freaking way!" Lisa said while looking at me in the rearview mirror.

"Oh my God! Did you tell anyone else this? He could've had something to do with Kristen Chambers going missing," Chelsea pointed out.

"Yes, she's right," Lisa agreed.

"Where is the diary? You got it with you?" Chelsea pressed me.

"No, I don't."

"Why not?" Chelsea wanted to know.

"Yeah, where is it?" Lisa added.

"The last time I had it with me was yesterday while I was washing my clothes in the laundry room. When I finished washing my things, I threw it in my laundry basket with my clothes and took them back up to my dorm room. Shortly after that, Tyler kicked in my door and attacked me. Jessica and Tyler's frat brother broke us up, and after everyone left, including Jessica, the diary went missing," I explained.

"From what you're saying, Tyler or his frat brother couldn't have taken it. Jessica might be the one who has it," Lisa said.

"But why would she take it?" Chelsea questioned.

"Did you tell her that you had it?" Lisa's questions continued.

"Yeah, in so many words."

"What do you mean? What did you say?" Chelsea asked.

"After reading a few entries from Gia's diary, I asked her if she recognized anything different about Gia. Or had Gia shared with her how badly her ex-boyfriend Scott was treating her, and she asked me where I was getting that from, and I told her."

"But why take it, though?" Chelsea probed me.

"That's what I keep asking myself too," I replied.

"Yes, something isn't right. Now Jessica would stay out all night and part of the morning," Lisa pointed out.

"I betcha when we get back to campus, she'll be in the dorm," Chelsea responded.

"Let's cross our fingers," I said.

Expecting the Unexpected

When Lisa, Chelsea, and I arrived back on campus, we all walked straight to my dorm. As we entered the first-floor lobby, I saw a couple of the residents I know and asked them if they'd seen Jessica. Penny spoke first.

"No, not since she left the dorm yesterday," she replied. "Is everything all right?"

"We'll soon find out," I replied as I got on the elevator.

I felt anxiety as it crept back into the pit of my stomach. My heart started beating faster. In my mind, all I wanted was to see Jessica when I entered my dorm room. She'd been gone since yesterday and I needed to see her so I knew that she was okay.

As the elevator door opened on my floor, I stepped off first. I headed in the direction of my room while Lisa and Chelsea followed me.

"Jessica, are you in here?" I asked aloud as I twisted the doorknob and pushed the door open. Anxious about seeing Jessica, I walked in the room. It was empty. I looked at her bed and behind the door, and she was nowhere in sight. This gave me a bad feeling. I looked back at Lisa and Chelsea as they entered the room.

"It looks like we may have to report her missing," Lisa suggested.

"Yes, I think you might be right," Chelsea agreed.

"Don't you think that we should call her parents first? What if she had to go home and forgot to tell us?" Lisa stated.

"Yeah, that's definitely a possibility," Chelsea agreed once more.

"Do you have her parents' number?" I asked.

"I've got her mother's number." Lisa answered first.

"Yeah, me too," Chelsea said.

"Lisa, call and see what they say," I instructed her, and then I took a seat on the edge of my bed while Chelsea sat on the edge of Jessica's bed. Lisa sat on the chair next to the desk after picking up the cordless telephone. It was apparent that no one wanted to sit on Gia's bed.

"It's ringing," Lisa said enthusiastically, and then she put the call on speaker.

"Hello," Jessica's mom said.

"Hi, Mrs. Vonn, this is Lisa, Jessica's friend. I am calling to ask you, have you spoken with Jessica since yesterday?"

Everyone waited for Mrs. Vonn to reply, but she was taking forever, so Lisa pushed her to answer.

"Hello, Mrs. Vonn, are you there?"

"Yes, I'm here. Please don't tell me that my baby is missing," she finally replied. She sounded out of it and instantly withdrawn. But who can blame her? One of her daughter's friends is calling and asking if she'd heard from her daughter.

"Mrs. Vonn, I am sitting here in Jessica's dorm room with her roommate Yoshi and her best friend Chelsea, and we have you on speakerphone. We have not seen Jessica since yesterday, and we've called everyone on campus that knows her, and everyone is saying that they haven't seen her. So we're calling you to see if you talked to or heard from her so that we won't draw our own conclusion and get everyone worked up for nothing."

"To answer your question, I haven't spoken to her since yesterday. She called me because she'd told me that she would call me back the night before."

"What time was this, if you don't mind me asking?" Lisa asked her.

"It was early in the afternoon."

"Did you ask her where she was or what she was doing?" Lisa's questions continued.

"As a matter of fact, I did. While we were talking, she sounded distracted, so I asked her what she was doing, and she told me that she was walking in the courtyard reading a book. I asked her what kind of book, and she said that it was a magazine. But then after a few minutes went by, I got her to talk about her day and she told me that a fight broke out with her roommate Yoshi and another person. I told her that I was sad to hear that. I even warned her about getting in the middle of something like that, because she could've gotten hurt."

"Did she say exactly where she was outside?"

"No. But later on in the conversation I started hearing a lot of guys in the background shouting and laughing, like she was at a party. And then a few minutes after that, I heard her close a door. From there, everything seemed to go completely quiet."

"How did you end the conversation?" Lisa pressed her.

"She said, 'Mama, let me call you back.' And then I told her that she better make sure she does, because she didn't call me back the previous day like she promised."

Listening to Mrs. Vonn give us details about her conversation with Jessica gave me an eerie feeling. What she just told us could not be made up. She told her mother that she was distracted because she was reading a book. And then she changed her mind and said that she was reading a magazine. But what was really creepy was how Mrs. Vonn heard a bunch of guys in the background making a ton of noise and then things went silent, which would explain the fact that Mrs. Vonn heard a door close. Was Jessica at the frat house with Gia's diary in hand?

"Mrs. Vonn, we're gonna give Jessica until tonight to come back to the dorm. If we don't see her or hear from her, we're gonna need you to file a missing person's report. But for now, we're gonna be optimistic and believe that she's okay and well," Lisa said.

"Have you called the hospitals? The police departments to see if she was at either of those places?" Mrs. Vonn asked.

"No, ma'am, we haven't. But that's what we're gonna do right now. And if we hear something, you will be the first person we call," Lisa assured her.

"I'm gonna talk to my Heavenly Father and have a discussion with Him while you girls try to find my daughter."

"You do just that, Mrs. Vonn," Lisa replied, and then she ended the call.

Immediately after Lisa hung up with Mrs. Vonn, she turned and looked at me and Chelsea. "From what Jessica's mom is saying, it sounds like she was at the frat house and she had the diary with her."

"I almost don't want to believe it, but it definitely sounds like where she was. Who knows, she may still be there. But the part that I'm grappling with is why take the diary with her?" I weighed in.

"I was asking myself that same question," Chelsea said.

"Come on, let's walk over there," Lisa suggested.

"I can't go. I have a restraining order against Tyler."

"What is it, like one hundred feet?" Lisa asked.

"Yes, but wait, Jessica has the same recorder as Dean

Paige. Get it from the second drawer on the left. You can use it to record your conversation when you get to the frat house," I mentioned.

"Okay, I'll take it with me. But you can still walk with us. Just sit on that park bench near the water fountain. You can still see good from that spot," Chelsea insisted.

"Yeah, Yoshi, Chelsea's right," Lisa agreed as she grabbed Jessica's handheld audio recorder.

"All right. Let's go," I said, and then we all exited my dorm room.

On our way back out the lobby, I noticed that Penny was still there hanging around and talking with the same girls she was talking to when we first arrived. I saw her through my peripheral vision trying to catch up with me as we headed to the front door that led to the outside. I was walking at a fast pace, but she was still able to catch up with me.

"Hey, is everything all right?" she asked, and began to walk alongside of me. She saw the intense look on my face, so it was quite obvious that something was wrong.

"I'm still looking for my roommate, Jessica," I told her.

"Oh no, that's not good," she replied while still trying to keep up with me. Lisa and Chelsea walked ahead of me.

"Yeah, I know. We just got off the phone with her mother, and she said that the last time she spoke to Jessica was yesterday, which was around the same time we last talked to her too."

"So where are you guys on your way to now?" Penny continued to question me.

"We're on our way to the frat house because her mom said that when she talked to Jessica, it sounded like Jessica was in a place where she heard a lot of guys in the background. So that's why we're headed over there."

"What are you going to say? And what if she isn't there?"

"Then we're gonna call every hospital and jail in the Tidewater area to see if they have her. I'm hoping that they do, because I can't lose another roommate."

"Now, don't jump to any conclusions. I'm sure that she will show up. Hopefully it'll be at the frat house," Penny said as she continued to walk beside me.

As we approached the bench where I was going to sit, Lisa and Chelsea looked back at me and told me that they were going to take things from there.

"Okay, but I'm watching you guys' every move," I assured them.

After Penny sat down next to me, she sparked up another Q&A session. "I truly hope that she's there. God knows that we don't need another missing person," she stated.

"I second that," I replied.

I watched as Lisa and Chelsea walked onto the front porch of the frat house, and the front door opened. Standing there were two random white guys looking like they were in the first stages of pledging and weren't quite frat brothers. I could tell that they were freshmen. I saw Lisa talking to them, and then one of them disappeared in the house. A minute or so later, the guy reappeared and had Conner with him. It looked like Lisa thanked the guy for getting Conner to come outside, and then the guy walked off.

I sat there on the bench and wished like hell that I could be there to listen to everything Conner was saying. But then I realized that I would in due time.

The conversation and interaction with them only lasted about three or four minutes, and then Lisa walked away. My heart skipped with every step she took.

Another Missing Person

After Lisa and Chelsea walked back to where I was sitting on the bench, they sat next to me, pulled out the recorder, and pressed play.

"Who are you guys looking for?" one of the guys asked.

"Is Tyler or Conner here?" Lisa answered.

"Tyler isn't, but Conner is," the same guy said.

"Would you get him for us?" Lisa replied.

"Sure," the guy said, and then I heard a door close.

A couple of seconds later, I heard the same door open.

"What's up?" I heard Conner say.

"We're looking for Jessica and no one has seen her since yesterday, so we were hoping that she was here," Lisa said.

"Well, she's not here," Conner said confidently. His tone sounded cocky too.

"When was the last time you seen her?" Chelsea chimed in.

"I don't know. Yesterday. Maybe the day before. I don't remember."

"What do you mean that you don't remember? No one has seen her since you and Tyler bum-rushed their dorm room yesterday. And you're telling me that it couldn't have been the day before yesterday."

"Yep, that's exactly what I'm saying. I don't keep up with her. She's not my girlfriend. She's sleeping with a couple of other dudes on campus, so go and ask them if they've seen her, because I haven't," Conner said sarcastically.

"You're such a fucking dickhead!" Lisa commented.

"Yeah, you really are," Chelsea weighed in.

"Hey, just know that you're not the first one to say that," he continued with his sarcasm.

"I'm telling you right now, if you're hiding anything concerning Jessica's whereabouts, you're gonna be sorry," Lisa threatened.

"Oh . . . woooooo, you're scaring me," he joked, and started quivering like he was afraid.

"Yeah, okay, keep showing off. I hope you have that same cockiness when they lock your ass up with a cell full of guys that's gonna treat you like you're their bitch!" Lisa roared.

I knew right then that she wasn't taking Jessica's unexpected disappearance very well. This bothered me too. To have her just up and vanish was mind-boggling. Where the fuck could she be?

"When your boss gets back to the house, let him know that we're onto him and that he's going down right with you."

"Yeah, right. You have nothing on us."

"That's not what Jessica's mom says. She said that Jessica told her that she was here yesterday, so who's lying?"

"She wasn't here. I don't know what her mom is talking about." Conner sounded shaky.

"Oh, don't worry, you will just as soon as everything falls into place," Lisa added, and then the recording stopped.

I felt devastated knowing that we just hit a brick wall. "Did you believe him?" I asked Lisa and Chelsea both.

"No, I didn't." Lisa answered first.

"You should've seen him up close. He didn't seem right," Chelsea said.

"I could tell by his voice that something was off. He knows where Jessica is," Penny chimed in.

"Think she might be dead?" Chelsea asked Penny.

"I can't say. I don't know Conner that well to make that call," Penny replied.

"But why would she be dead? What could she possibly do for someone to do that to her?" Lisa asked us all.

"I don't know," I finally said.

"We need to stop jumping to conclusions and get on the phone and call all the hospitals and county jails to see if they have her," Penny suggested.

"That was the next thing we were going to do, so let's do it," I added.

"Where should we go?" Chelsea wanted to know.

"Let's go back to my dorm room," I offered. I felt it would be better, being that I had the space. Neither Gia nor Jessica was with us right now, so what better place to get the energy to find Jessica than in the room where she lived?

Back in my dorm room, Chelsea, Lisa, and Penny sat down wherever they could, and we placed calls to every police precinct, county jail, hospital, urgent care facility, and shelter, but Jessica was not anywhere. We even asked if they had seen her, and again, everyone said no. This gave me a sick feeling in the pit of my stomach. We all knew that it was time to file a missing person's report on Jessica. The one thing I dreaded was calling her mother back, so I gave that job to Lisa.

Like the first time, all of us sat in a circle while Lisa called Jessica's mother and put the call on speakerphone.

"Hello?"

"Hi, Mrs. Vonn, this is Lisa, Jessica's friend from ODU. I called you earlier about Jessica. . . ."

"Yes."

"Okay, so her friends and I are all sitting in her dorm room and wanted to call you back and let you know that we still haven't found her and that, with your permission, we want to file a missing person's report," Lisa stated.

"Did you call the police stations and the hospitals?" she wanted to know.

"Yes, ma'am, we have all called every place that she could go," Lisa added.

"Well, let me put my husband on the phone, because he's good at talking about stuff like this. See, I'm sixty-five years old. Jessica isn't my child. I'm really her grandmother. I took her when her mother died after giving birth to her. So hold on and let me put Harold on the phone."

While Mrs. Vonn was getting her husband, everyone in the room looked at each other because we never knew that her mother was actually her grandmother.

"I was wondering why she had delayed reactions to everything I was telling her in the first phone call. She's an old lady," Lisa pointed out after putting the call on mute.

"Young lady, are you still here?" she asked Lisa.

Lisa deactivated the mute button. "Yes, ma'am, I'm still here," Lisa told her.

"Okay, I'm putting my husband on the phone right now," she informed us.

"Hello," I heard the man say.

"Hi, Mr. Vonn, my name is Lisa. I called earlier and told your wife that Jessica has gone missing and . . ."

"What do you mean 'gone missing'?" he asked, cutting Lisa off midsentence.

"'day, and this is not like her to just disappear without telling someone where she is," Lisa was finally able to explain.

"Did you call the hospital?"

"Yes, sir. We've called the hospital, emergency room, clinics, and police stations, and there's no record of her going to those places."

"So you said that you need me and my wife to file a missing person's report?" he asked Lisa.

Listening to Jessica's grandparents communicating with Lisa told me that they were much older and didn't know how to navigate around certain things and would probably need to appoint a power of attorney for themselves in another year or so. It wouldn't surprise me if they had hearing aids or walked with a cane.

"Yes, sir," Lisa replied.

"How do we do that? Is there a phone number that we call?" he continued as his voice fluctuated.

"Yes, we have a number that you can call," Lisa told him.

"Okay, well, let me get a pen and a piece of paper," he said. We all heard him fumbling around with something in the background. "Okay, you can go ahead," he continued after he got back on the phone.

"The number I am giving you is the Missing Person's Unit of the Norfolk Police Department. The phone number is 342-555-0110."

"You said 342 . . . 555 . . . 0110?" he repeated.

"Yes," Lisa agreed.

"And that number is the Missing Person's Department at the police station?" He wanted clarity.

"Yes," Lisa replied.

"So what I do is call that number and tell him that my granddaughter is missing and that I want to take out a report on her?"

"Yes, sir, that's exactly what you say. And also say that she was last seen yesterday," Lisa told him.

"Is her car still at the school?" he asked.

"Yes, it's still parked on campus. So let them know that too."

"Okay, I will do that," he assured her.

"Call me back as soon as you're done talking to the missing person's investigative."

"The who?" He wanted Lisa to repeat herself.

"The missing person's police guy. Call me when you're done speaking with him."

"Is this your number our telephone?"

"Yes, sir, it is."

"Okay. As soon as I talk to the police, I will call you back."

"Thank you so much."

"You're welcome," he said, and then the call went radio silent.

"Oh my God! I feel so sorry for them." Chelsea spoke first.

"I know, me too," I chimed in.

"Has Jessica ever mentioned that she was raised by her grandparents?" Lisa asked the group.

"No," Chelsea said.

"She never mentioned it," I added. Penny just sat back because she didn't know Jessica like we did.

"So what do we do now?" I asked the group.

"We just sit around and wait," Chelsea replied.

"You know that you can file a missing person's report too?" Penny announced.

Everyone turned their attention toward her.

"We can?" I asked.

"Yes. You can go down to the precinct or call. But I think doing it in person would add a sudden urgency to it," Penny explained.

"Okay, I'm ready. So let's go," I instructed the girls. Everyone but Chelsea stood up. "You guys are gonna have to go without me," she said.

"Why? What's the matter?" I asked her.

"I've got to retake my exam tonight. If I don't go, I'll get a zero," she told us.

"Don't worry. We understand," I replied for the whole group. "One of us will let you know what happens after we file the report," I assured her.

It was only Lisa, me, and Penny heading down to the precinct to file a missing report on Jessica. While we were leaving campus, it was Penny's idea to get Jessica's license plate number off her car. So we walked over to student parking to do just that, but Jessica's car wasn't there.

"Is it me, or am I seeing things?" I pointed out.

"What's wrong?" Penny asked first.

"Jessica's car isn't here?" Lisa noticed.

"Where could it be?" I said aloud.

"What if she has it? What if she's not missing?" Lisa said optimistically.

"It's a possibility," Penny chimed back in.

"I would love for that to be true," I replied.

"I guess time will tell," Lisa added, and then we headed to her car.

The ride to the police station didn't take long. As soon as we arrived, Penny insisted that we go inside the precinct without her because she needed to use the pay phone outside. We obliged her and went inside the police station without her. After filling out the necessary information on Jessica's missing person's report, a cop met with Lisa and me less than ten minutes later. This time I spoke with a female investigator. She was a young black Afrocentric-looking woman who looked like she didn't tolerate any mess. If I had to say so myself, she looked like a young version of Erika Alexander without all the face and hair jewelry. She introduced herself as Detective Richards, and then she escorted Lisa and me back to her office.

After we took a seat, she looked over the information I put

on paper and then she looked back at Lisa and me and started asking questions.

"I take it you filled out this missing report?" she asked me.

"Yes," I said.

"And you are?" she asked as she looked at Lisa.

"My name is Lisa."

"How are you ladies related to Jessica Vonn?" the detective asked us.

"She's our friend," Lisa answered.

"She's my roommate," I added.

"She's a black female with light brown eyes, shoulder length blond hair. Is blond her natural hair color?"

"No. She had it dyed. Her normal color is dark brown," I replied.

"I see that she's five foot five and roughly one hundred twenty pounds."

"Yes."

"Do you have a photo of her?"

"Yes, I do," I said, and grabbed the only picture I had of her, when we were at the carnival a few months back.

"Great. Thank you," she replied. "Do you know the year, make, model, and color of her car?"

"It's a red four-door Honda Accord. I don't know the year though," I stated.

"I don't know the year either. But I do know that it's almost new," Lisa said.

"By any chance would either of you have a photo of the last guy she was seeing?"

"No," Lisa pointed out.

"I forgot to ask, does she have any visible marks or tattoos on her body?"

"Yes, she has her first name written in Asian letters on her right wrist," I replied.

"Is it big? Small?"

"It's about two inches long," I added.

"I see she's from Richmond."

"Yes, ma'am," I agreed.

"Have you two contacted her family? Mom? Dad?"

"Yes, Lisa and I both spoke to her grandparents. We gave her grandfather the phone number to call here too. I'm not sure if he's done it yet," I said.

"So she's been missing for at least twenty-four hours?"

"Yes, ma'am," I replied. Lisa sat back and watched.

"Where was the last place you saw her?"

"In our dorm room. When I lay down to take a nap, she was there. When I woke up, she was gone and I haven't spoken or seen her since," I stated.

"Same here. I saw her earlier in the day, and then I haven't talked to her since," Lisa answered.

"Have you tried to call her?"

"Of course we have. I've called her so many times, I lost count," I told her.

"I called her a lot too. But it just goes straight to voice mail," Lisa said.

"Does Jessica have a boyfriend?"

"No, not really. She doesn't like to put labels on things. But I can say that she was sleeping with one of the frat guys on campus named Conner," I told the cop.

"Where is he now?" the cop wanted to know.

"He lives on campus in the frat house," I added.

"Think he'll be there now if I take a ride over there?"

"I'm sure he will," I responded.

"Does Jessica have any enemies?"

"No," I said.

"Not that I know of," Lisa answered.

"Did she date any other guys?"

"See, Jessica is a free spirit, so she could be with one guy one day and then two days later she's with another guy."

"Does she have a car?"

"Yes, she does. And what's so crazy is that we saw it

parked in the student parking lot on the day she went missing. But right before we came here, it was gone. Now tell me how that happened?"

"Is there a possibility that she could've moved it?"

"If she had, she would've come to our dorm room first," I assured her. "Someone other than her moved it. I can almost guarantee it," I continued.

"Who?" the cop pressed.

"That's the thing, I don't know," I answered.

"Neither do I," Lisa said.

"Another ODU student disappeared months ago. Do you think that this incident could be connected?" I asked the detective.

"I can't say for sure, but there's a possibility that they could be linked. I will look into that," she insisted.

"Can you tell me how long this process works, and when do you start searching for her?" I wanted to know.

"I'm gonna get the ball rolling immediately after I enter this information in the system. So if there is nothing else you can think of, I'm gonna go and move things along now."

I sat there for a moment trying to figure out if me telling this detective that Jessica could be in possession of Gia's diary would help. In my mind, a part of me says that whoever has Jessica has possession of Gia's diary too.

"I do have something else to say."

"What is it?" the detective asked.

"The day she went missing, she had a diary with her that belonged to our other roommate, Gia, who passed away from an overdose recently. I had the diary in my possession but for some reason or another Jessica took it and vanished with it."

"What was in the diary?"

"My roommate Gia wrote about how she'd been hurt physically and mentally by her then boyfriend Scott," I started off saying. "You're familiar with the missing girl Kristen Chambers, right?" I added.

"Yes, I'm the lead investigator on that case too."

"Well, in the diary, Gia wrote about seeing Kristen Chambers the night she went missing," I told her.

"Did she say where?"

"Yes, she said that Kristen was hanging outside of the frat house talking to Tyler. He's the president of that chapter."

"Did she say anything else?"

"I looked for more entries about Kristen, but when I sifted through the pages I noticed that there were some pages torn from it," I told her.

"And you say that Jessica is in possession of this?"

"Yes, ma'am."

"When did you come in contact with this diary?"

"A day after Gia died in the hospital. Her parents wanted me to pack her things, so I did and that's when I found it," I explained.

"It didn't occur to you to turn that diary in to the local authorities?"

"Yeah, it did. But after I read it, I guess."

"If you happen to find it, please call me, because that diary may have some very important information that could help solve the other missing persons case, and hopefully it'll direct us to where Jessica is."

I nodded my head.

Lisa and I stood up from our chairs and shook the detective's hand. We thanked her, and then she handed us her card. It felt good to do our part in finding Jessica. All we had to do then was find out who had her car.

Carjacking

When Lisa and I exited the police station, Penny was leaning against Lisa's passenger side door looking at the sky. "You guys done?" she asked us.

"Yes, we are," I answered.

Lisa made her way around to the driver's side of her car and then she crawled inside.

"So, who did you speak with?" Penny's questions started.

"A black lady named Detective Richards. She took all the information she needed to start the search and gave us her business card, so if we need to call her, we can. She also said that she's gonna send out an alert for Jessica's car. If we don't find out who has it, then I'm sure she will," I stated.

"She will," Penny assured us. "So what are we gonna do now?" she added.

"There's really nothing for us to do. I mean, we could ride around town and look for her car," I suggested.

"I'm down," Lisa said.

"Me too. But while we're out, it would be wise to have fly-ers with a picture of her face. That way we can post them or give them out," Penny replied.

"Yeah, she's right," I agreed.

"I'll tell you what. Lisa, you can take me to student parking so I can hop in my car and Yoshi and I can ride around through the different neighborhoods in Norfolk to see if we can locate Jessica's car while you make the flyers."

"Okay, I'm cool with that," Lisa replied.

"Great. Then let's get to it," Penny said with enthusiasm even though we were faced with the challenge of looking for someone we saw as family. I could only hope that our plan worked.

As soon as we arrived in student parking, Lisa parked her car so she could go to her dorm room, and Penny and I went to her car. We hopped into a white Volkswagen Bug. It was really cute on the inside, with a rainbow-colored cartoon Barney attached to the middle air conditioner vent. Then she had a bobblehead of Scooby-Doo on the dashboard. She also had a Wonder Woman figurine hanging from her rearview mirror, and the entire car smelled like it was brand new.

"I see you're a fan of cartoons," I commented as she started the ignition.

"Yes, ever since I was a child," she responded.

"So where are we going first?" I asked her as she drove out of the parking lot and onto the main street of the campus.

"I was thinking we could start looking in the Park Place area."

"I think so too, since it's just a couple of streets over from campus," I agreed. "Think we'll find her car?"

"I hope so. It'll be devastating to know that someone took another one of our female students from campus. Or anywhere else, for that matter."

As planned, we drove around all the neighborhoods in Norfolk looking for Jessica's car, but we couldn't find it parked anywhere. I figured that the likelihood of finding her car that night was impossible. This made me sick to my stomach. Damn, I wished I knew where she was. I didn't think that I was gonna be able to sit around and not do anything while someone was holding my roommate against her will.

"So I guess it's back to the campus we go," I said as I stared out of the passenger side window.

"Listen, Yoshi, I have a confession to make," Penny said as she pulled her car to the side of the road.

Hearing the word *confession* instantly gave me anxiety. I didn't know whether to listen to what she had to say or get out of her car. What did I have to lose?

After she put her car in park, she looked at me. But before I gave her a chance to utter one word, I said, "Please don't tell me that you had something to do with Jessica's disappearance, because I don't know how I am going to take it."

"No, that's not what I am going to say."

Boy, was I relieved to hear those words. I took a deep breath and then I exhaled. "So, what is it?"

She reached in her pocket, pulled out a black leather wallet, and then turned it around. She was holding a detective badge.

"You're a cop?" I asked her. I pretty much knew that she was going to say yes, but hearing the words come from her mouth made more sense to me. I needed confirmation.

"I am actually a detective in the Special Victims Unit," she replied.

"So are you a detective *and* a student?"

"No, I'm just a law enforcement agent."

"So, what, am I about to get arrested?"

"No, Yoshi."

"So, why are you telling me that you're a detective? I don't understand."

"I was sent here to investigate the disappearance of Kristen Chambers, and while I was doing that, Gia dies of an overdose and now Jessica is missing. And the reason why I am telling you this is because I need your help finding Jessica. See, I know that she has Gia's diary in her possession, because she was supposed to bring it to me."

"Okay, wait, I'm confused. How did you know the diary even existed in the first place?"

"Jessica told me that you found the diary. And she told me that Gia said something about seeing Kristen standing outside the frat house on the night she disappeared."

"I read that. I told Jessica that," I said.

"She mentioned that."

"Why didn't she just ask me for the diary? Or told me that you wanted it?"

"Because I told her not to."

"How did you convince her to steal it from me?"

"Yoshi, Jessica was busted not that long ago buying drugs from Rita Reznik, the campus drug dealer. So after Jessica made the buy a month ago, I gave her the choice of squeezing information out of anyone who knew Kristen Chambers or go to jail. She chose to be my informant."

"What did you do with Rita? Is she your informant too?"

"Not yet. But she will be after tonight. She knows a lot of students on campus, so I know that she can steer me in the right direction."

"How will you get her to flip?"

"When I tell her how much time she would face for selling drugs on school grounds, she'll start singing like a bird."

"Do you have any ideas where Jessica could be? And do you think that you'll ever find Kristen?"

"I have a couple of sources that say Tyler Egan and a few of his frat brothers know where she is, which is why I encouraged Jessica to hang out at the frat house more. When she started spending a lot of time with Conner, I became somewhat concerned when I noticed her getting emotionally invested with that guy."

"I wondered why she would still go over there after Tyler raped me. Now it makes sense."

"FYI, she's on the fence about Tyler raping you. I believe Conner got in her ear. But I know the look of a rape victim, and that night I saw you running back to the dorm. Too bad I didn't catch you in time, because I would've driven you to the hospital myself to get that rape exam performed."

"I appreciate you saying that."

"So what will it be? Gonna help me find her or what?"

"Do you think that Tyler got something to do with Jessica missing right now?"

"That's a huge possibility."

"Well, let's do it," I agreed.

Risking It All

Processing all the information that Penny just laid on me was a lot to absorb. Who would've known that Penny was a freaking undercover cop all this time? I was a good judge of character, so how come I didn't pick that up? On top of that, how come I didn't pick up that Jessica had turned snitch? How was she able to walk around and interact with suspects that could be involved with Kristen Chambers's disappearance? I know one thing, it would bring me so much joy to bust Tyler's ass and see him taken in custody by Penny for any involvement of any wrongdoing on campus. He needs to go once and for all.

Immediately after we arrived back on campus, Penny parked her car and went into search mode. "I've got to find Rita Reznik, and I'm gonna need your help doing it," Penny said after getting out of her car.

"How do we propose to do that?" I asked after she locked her car doors.

"I want you to call her and tell her that you want to spend some money with her."

"Wait, you want me to call her and tell her that I wanna buy drugs from her?" I asked as I stood next to the trunk of her car.

"Yep," she replied as she stood before me.

"Do you know how that's gonna look when she finds out that I set her up? Do you know who her father and brother are?"

"From your tone I can only guess that they're drug dealers too," she commented.

"You're fucking right they are, and I don't wanna get involved," I insisted.

"Oh wait," Penny said as she turned her attention four hundred yards away in the north part of the courtyard.

When I followed her eyes, I realized that she was looking at Rita. Rita was standing at least one hundred feet away from my dorm. It was clear she was swapping money for drugs because of the hand movement like an exchange had taken place.

"Hey, Rita, let me holler at you for a second!" Penny shouted as she waved her hand at Rita. It was ten at night, so the courtyard wasn't a complete ghost town.

"Who is that?" Rita shouted back.

"It's Yoshi and Penny."

"Why did you say my name?" I questioned. I'd just told her that I didn't want to be the middleman for her and Rita.

Without saying another word, Rita started walking toward us, and Penny started walking in her direction.

"Come on, let's go." Penny looked back and instructed me.

Feeling an enormous amount of pressure, I reluctantly followed Penny to meet up with Rita.

"What's up?" Rita asked Penny after they were within two feet of each other. I was a ways from them—about one hundred feet, to be exact—and Rita noticed and mentioned it.

"We're trying to get a couple of opioids or a gram or two of coke," Penny replied.

"Opioids? Coke? No one on this campus says 'opioids.' So I'm gonna ask you, Who the hell are you? And Yoshi, I need to know why you're way back there? You know I can't do business with you while you're a hundred feet away," Rita responded sarcastically. She definitely knew that something wasn't right.

"My name is Penny. You've seen me around campus. And I meant to say Xanax. You know, whatever you got." Penny tried to clean up her mess. She knew that Rita was on to her.

"Yoshi, I'm gonna need you to walk faster toward me so you can tell me who the fuck is this girl?"

"She lives in my dorm," I told Rita as I approached them both.

"I don't care where she lives at. Who is she? And why she asking me for 'opioids'? Or coke? She sounds like a straight cop if you ask me," Rita said. I could see skepticism written all over her face.

"Look, you see me on this campus all the time, so you wanna make some money or what?" Penny fired back at her. I couldn't believe how cocky she had just gotten.

"Seeing you around campus doesn't mean that you ain't a cop. So if y'all need something, then I'm only dealing with Yoshi," she told Penny, and then she turned her attention toward me. By this time, I was within arm's length of her. "What'cha need, Yoshi?" Rita asked me as if Penny weren't there.

I paused for a moment because I had no idea what to say. There I was standing between a drug dealer and a cop, unaware about what was going to happen immediately after Rita and I exchanged money for drugs. What must I do?

"Look, I don't have all night. Wanna get your usual or what?" Rita pressed me.

"Yes, give her the usual," Penny instructed Rita.

"Is that what you want?" Rita wanted clarity.

"Yeah," I said, not realizing that I'd opened my mouth.

Seconds later, Rita reached in her pocket and grabbed a labelless medicine bottle. After she unscrewed the cap, she dumped a couple of pills in the palm of her hand and then handed them to me. She gave me four pills in total—four Xanax.

"Give her one hundred dollars," I told Penny.

"No, I'm not accepting money from her. She's gonna give it to you and then you give it to me," Rita insisted.

"Okay, fine," Penny agreed, and handed the money to me and then I handed it to Rita.

After the transaction concluded, Penny pulled out her badge, damn near shoved it in Rita's face, and told her that she was under arrest. Rita tried to make a run for it, but Penny grabbed her and pinned her arms behind her back.

"Get the fuck off me!" Rita ranted as she tussled with Penny. For a minute there, I thought Rita was going to overpower Penny because she was so much bigger, but whatever training Penny got from the police academy enabled her to put Rita's face in the dirt, literally.

"Rita, you have the right to remain silent. Anything you say can and will be used against you in a court of law. You have a right to an attorney and have him present with you when being questioned. If you cannot afford one, one will be appointed to you before any questioning. Do you understand these rights I have explained to you?" Penny asked.

"Fuck you! I don't give a damn about no rights. Yoshi, you sold me out. You're a snitch now?!" Rita spat as Penny placed a plastic zip tie on her.

"You better close your mouth before I blow the whistle on you. I will pull out my bullhorn and let the entire campus know that you're the campus drug dealer, and if that happens, the word will surely get back to the dean and Student Affairs. From there, you'll be kicked out of school, charged with possession of an illegal substance and distribution. That alone will you put in jail for five years. When you come home from doing time, you'll be put on parole, no one will hire a convicted felon, you won't be able to get back in school, and you won't be able to vote. So tell me, how do you want this to play out?" Penny responded as she helped Rita sit on the curb next to where her car was parked.

"How does it feel to be a snitch?" Rita asked me as she gritted her teeth.

"She actually didn't snitch on you. Remember when Jessica bought ten Xanax and two grams of coke from you not too long ago? I saw the whole transaction. I could've arrested you back then, but Jessica begged me not to. So count your lucky stars."

"So what'cha want from me? You want me to set up the dude I get my supply from?" Rita said.

"No, that won't be necessary," Penny said.

"Then what do you want?" Rita wanted to know.

"I want you to tell me how often you go to the frat house and who spends the most money," Penny asked her.

Rita looked at me. "You're trying to railroad Tyler, huh?" she asked me.

"No, this right here doesn't have anything to do with me. She's here because Jessica is missing and she believes that the guys at the frat house know where she is. I mean, didn't you tell me to go to the frat house earlier?" I reminded her.

Rita took in what I said, and then she turned her attention back toward Penny. "If you're trying to get me to say that Tyler is my biggest customer, I can't because we never exchanged money. He gets the guys that live with him to do it. If I don't deal with Conner, he gets Eric to do it."

"When was the last time you sold to them?" Penny asked.

"Today. Conner called me to come over there. And when I

got there, he told me he needed twenty Xannies, so I handed them to him and he gave me four hundred dollars. After we made the deal, I left," Rita explained.

"How do you know that he was buying them for Tyler?" Penny probed more.

"Because I've witnessed Conner or Eric buying from me and then handing the drugs to Tyler," Rita stated.

"Do you believe that Tyler raped me?" I interjected. I needed someone to tell me that I wasn't crazy. That I wasn't trying to railroad Tyler because we had a one-night stand. I needed to hear someone tell me that they believed me.

Rita turned her attention back toward me. "Everybody in that frat house knows that Tyler raped you. But they will never go against him and tell you that," Rita pointed out.

"See, I told you," I commented as I swung at the air. It felt so liberating to hear someone say that they believed me.

"Yoshi, I never doubted you. I told you, I knew something happened when I saw you running back to the dorm," Penny assured me.

I started to say something, but I choked up. Instead, my eyes became watery.

"Rita, I'm gonna need you to set up a buy with Conner. If we catch him with his pants down, he'll tell us where Jessica is." Penny laid out the plan.

"That's not gonna work," Rita replied.

"Why not?" Penny wanted to know.

"Because they call me. I don't call them."

"She's got a point," I mentioned.

"Tell you what, call him and tell him that you got some coke that you want him and his boys to try out. And if they like it, for the first buy, they can get it for half price," Penny explained.

"That's a good plan," I chimed in.

Rita thought for a second and then said, "Yeah, a'ight, I can do that."

"Great!" Penny seemed pleased. "Now, I'm gonna untie you, so don't do anything stupid," Penny warned her.

"Trust me, I won't try to make a run for it. Just get me out of this thing before someone sees me like this," Rita told Penny.

"Okay, but be a woman of your word," Penny reminded her, and then she cut the zip tie from Rita's wrists.

Rita stood up and started massaging her wrists. She even complained about how tight the tie was. But I wasn't concerned about that. I was waiting for her to sprint off in the opposite direction, but she didn't. She kept her word and called Conner from the nearest pay phone. We moved in close to hear.

"Hello," we all heard him say.

"Hey, this is Rita and I've got a proposition for you."

"What's up?" he asked, seeming curious.

"I just got some new stuff that I want you and the boys to try out."

"Nah, we're good. We still have a few pills left from the last time," Conner said.

"Conner, I'm not selling them. I'm giving a couple of them away. And if you like them, then the next buy would be full price," Rita suggested.

"I don't know. . . ." he said, seeming unsure about what to do. "You know that I don't really do the stuff myself. Tyler gets me or Eric to cop from you for him and the girls he brings over," Conner continued. And while he was talking, I felt my blood beginning to boil.

"You don't use any of that stuff you get from me?" Rita asked him.

"Sometimes. But not as often as Tyler and Eric."

"Look, I'm gonna bring a couple of these things by, and all you need to do is give them to Tyler. Tell 'im it's a gift from me because of all the money you guys have been spending with me," Rita added.

Boy, was this girl a natural. It almost felt like she was talking to me. If she called me with that proposal, I knew I would take it.

After Rita convinced Conner to meet with her, he insisted that we meet him outside the campus store because he was on his way there. Rita agreed, and we were off to the races.

"Good job, Rita!" Penny said. I could tell that she was pleased with how Rita handled that situation with Conner.

"If we're gonna do this, let's go now," Rita insisted.

"I'm ready," Penny told her.

He's Evil!

I wanted to be there when Rita sealed the deal with Conner, but I knew that I couldn't show my face. Conner would've seen the red flag immediately and know that something was off, and then he would bail on us before we got a chance to railroad him.

"Let me get my wire from my car," Penny said.

Rita and I watched Penny as she walked to the trunk of her car. Within a matter of fifteen seconds, she opened the trunk, grabbed a small black box, and then was standing front and center attaching the wire to Rita's jacket.

"I'm using this particular wire to get footage and record sound that I won't be able to hear with my naked ear. So don't move it. Understood?"

"Okay, I got it. I'm ready to blow this place. I've got shit to do," Rita whined.

"You can walk ahead of me. I'll be a few feet behind you."

"And I'll stay behind you, Penny," I mentioned.

"Yes, you stay behind me," Penny agreed.

Seconds later, Rita walked off and headed in the direction

of the campus library. Penny waited for about two minutes and then followed the direction Rita was taking. I got on the train a couple of minutes after Penny. Like Penny, I had to appear invisible.

While following Penny, I knew that I had to stand about fifty feet away from Rita and Conner when he exited the library, but I kept my back to them. I pretended to be looking for a book and had my peripheral vision working overtime. From my angle, I could see Rita hand Conner the drugs as she was instructed to do. He looked down into the palm of his hand and then he looked back at Rita. They exchanged words, he closed his hand, and then he walked away from her. Immediately after Conner walked away, Penny rushed over to Rita and took the wiring device from her. After she had the wire recorder in hand, she waved and motioned for me to follow her, so I did.

Rita walked off. I didn't know whether Penny gave her permission to leave or not, but Rita was in the wind. I guessed Penny would take care of her later.

While Conner headed in the direction of the frat house, Penny started walking behind Conner. She noticed that he was walking quickly and that she wouldn't catch up with him unless she walked faster. Even that didn't work, so she yelled his name.

"Excuse me, Conner," I heard her say to get his attention. And what do you know? Calling his name did it.

Conner stopped and turned around. He stood there and waited to see what Penny wanted. She finally caught up with him, and I was only a few feet behind them.

"Conner, my name is Penny. How are you doing?" Penny started her conversation off.

"I'm doing fine. But I'm in a rush right now, so what can I do for you?" He seemed nervous.

"You don't remember me from hanging around on campus?"

"Yeah, I've seen you a couple of times, why?"

"Because my name is Penny Nelson, and you're under arrest for possession of an illegal substance." Penny showed her law enforcement badge to him as she spoke.

By this time, I was standing side by side with Penny. "You're what? And I'm what?" he responded. He was surely confused.

"You're under arrest for possession of illegal drugs. Now turn around and put your arms behind you," Penny instructed him.

Judging from Conner's facial expression, I thought that he was going to make a run for it, but surprisingly he didn't.

"You set me up?" he asked me.

"No, dummy. You did this to yourself."

"Turn around before I make a scene and let everyone out here know what I am arresting you for," Penny threatened him.

Penny grabbed Conner's arms and strapped a zip tie to his wrists. Once that was done, she took the prescription drugs from his hand and slid them down into her front pants pocket.

"Are we gonna stand right here?" he wanted to know.

"Are you telling me that you don't want to be here?" Penny asked.

"I don't want anyone walking by and seeing me like this. Word will get around campus, and I don't want that kind of heat," he explained.

"Well, let's move over here," Penny said as she pointed to a green metal box on the side of the library. There was a small light there, but it was also a dead end. No thru traffic.

"Don't give him any special treatment," I interjected. I wanted him to suffer just like I suffered when I was railroaded by him and his frat brother. Not only was I embarrassed on the night of my rape, they also humiliated me in the courtyard when Tyler grabbed me by my neck and lifted me off my feet. Conner stood there and laughed. Now see who gets the last laugh.

"Mind your business," he grumbled.

"Conner, be quiet so I can read you your rights."

"You're really arresting me?" he asked.

"Yes. Conner, you have the right to remain silent. Anything you say can and will be used against you in a court of law. You have a right to an attorney and have him present with you when being questioned. If you cannot afford one, one will be appointed to you before any questioning. Do you understand these rights I have explained to you?" Penny asked.

"Yes, but is there something I can do to prevent this from happening?" he added.

"What do you have in mind?" Penny probed him. But she knew where he was going with this. This loser knows that if he gives up his partners in crime, he could get out of this jam. He was the most spineless guy that I'd ever laid my eyes on.

"I don't know. What can I do? What do you need? Want me to set my frat brothers up and trick them into buying drugs?" he proposed.

"No, that's not gonna do it for me." Penny toyed with his mind. I stood there disgusted.

"Where is Jessica?" Penny asked him, and she looked him dead in the eye.

I swear, this guy looked like a deer in headlights. He wasn't ready for that question. She completely caught him off guard. Even though I couldn't see it, I know he was sweating bullets underneath his shirt.

"What do you mean, where is Jessica? I don't know," he answered. But Penny and I both knew that he was lying.

"Answer my question. Where is Jessica? I know you know

where she is. Now if you don't tell me right now, I am going to charge you with possession of an illegal substance and distribution. That alone will put you in prison for ten years. And while you're in prison, one of those convicts is going to make you their bitch! They're going to bend you over and rape you. And if you make it out of prison, you'll be put on parole. No one will hire a convicted felon, you won't be able to get back in school, and you won't be able to vote. So tell me, how do you want this to play out?" Penny responded.

Conner must've gotten terrified over the idea of being someone's prison bitch and told Penny what he knew.

"She's in the trunk of her car," he finally answered.

"What do you mean by that? Is she dead or alive?" Penny wanted to know.

Right now, my anxiety kicked back in full force after hearing Conner tell us that Jessica was in the trunk of her car. I was afraid to hear what else he had to say, but I knew that I couldn't go anywhere, so I stood there.

"She's dead," he replied.

There it was, the words that I dreaded to hear. This couldn't be true. I had just seen her less than forty-eight hours ago. And now she was dead? I couldn't lose two friends in the same month. How was I going to cope?

"Who killed her? You fucking rat! I fucking hate you," I roared, and started kicking Conner in the chest and shoulders. Anywhere I could get a kick in. He blocked a couple of blows I sent his way. But that didn't matter, I just wanted to hurt him wherever I could.

After I hit him a few times, Penny grabbed me and pulled me away from him.

"Yoshi, calm down. I got this," Penny said, trying to settle me down. She finally got me to calm down after holding me for a minute and whispering in my ear that she would get justice for Jessica.

"I didn't kill her," Conner announced.

"Then who did?" Penny asked him.

"Tyler," he replied.

"Why?" Penny pressed him.

"Because I told Tyler that she kept asking me questions about the missing girl, Kristen Chambers."

"What questions was she asking you?"

"She asked me did we know her? Had she ever come to the frat house? And did I think that she was still alive?"

"He killed her over that?" I chimed in. My poor heart was hurting.

"No, he decided that he wanted to get rid of her because I told him that Jessica had Gia's diary and that it said that Kristen was standing outside on the night she went missing. So Tyler thought it would be best that I get rid of her because she was a loose end. But I couldn't get up the nerve to kill her. I'm not built like that. So he did it himself," Conner stated.

"How did he kill her?" Penny asked, wanting more details.

"He choked her until she couldn't breathe anymore."

"Fucking bastard!" I snapped, and then I lunged at Conner. I mean, how in the hell could he have allowed Tyler to do that to Jessica? He was screwing her brains out on the regular. Doesn't that account for something?

Penny had to pull me off Conner again while he was trying to dodge my kicks.

"Yoshi, please stop. I'm gonna make them pay for what they did to Jessica. So let me do my job," she said softly. "Where is the diary? Does he have it?" Penny's questions continued.

"Yeah, he has it in his room."

"Let's get back to Kristen Chambers. Was she at the frat house the night she disappeared?" Penny pressured him.

"Yes," he answered.

"Who was she there to see?"

"Tyler. He invited her over to the house. When she got

there, they chilled out, drank a little, and then he tried to drug her. She saw him put some powder in her drink and went off on him. She started calling him desperate and said he was a loser, and he didn't like it. So he beat her up a little and then he suffocated her with one of his pillows."

Hearing about yet another girl being killed at the hands of Tyler made my heart heavy. I was angry and I was sad for the parents of this young woman. The way Tyler used, abused, and discarded their bodies was unfathomable. If I had a gun and he was in my face right now, I would shoot him right through the head.

"Where is Kristen's body right now?" Penny wanted to know.

"It's buried in the basement of the frat house. We were getting the basement repaved with concrete anyway, so Tyler thought that it would be better to bury her there. This way we wouldn't get caught carrying her body out of the house."

"Are you sure of this?" Penny wanted confirmation.

"Yes, I'm sure. I was there playing lookout when Tyler and Eric dug up the hole and placed her body in it."

"Conner, are you willing to testify in front of judge and jury with this information that you've just given me about the murders of Jessica Vonn and Kristen Chambers?" Penny asked him.

"Yes," he said.

"Well, so you know, I've recorded our interview and will use it as evidence against the persons of interest involving the two women whose lives were taken," Penny stated. "For the record, Conner, can you tell me where Jessica's car is?" Penny added.

"Eric and I drove it to the Dismal Swamp in Virginia Beach near Indian River Road."

"Who drove it there?"

"I drove it there. Eric drove his car, so after the car went in the water, I got in Eric's car and we came back to the frat house together."

"Conner, you're a piece of shit! You know that?" I gritted my teeth at him.

"Do you know the area? Would you be able to take us right to it?" Penny's questions kept coming.

"Yes, I'm sure I can," he insisted.

"Come on, let's go," Penny said, and then she helped him onto his feet. He stood there with his arms still behind his back, looking around to see if someone spotted him.

"So what's gonna happen now?" he wanted to know.

"I'm gonna put you in my car while I wait for backup," she informed him, and then she escorted him back to her car. I followed just to make sure that he didn't try to run off, all while hurt and sick to my stomach that Jessica was dead, thrown in the trunk of her car and buried in a nasty and disgusting swamp. These guys were freaking monsters and I would make sure Jessica got justice for what they did to her.

After Penny put Conner in her car, she locked the doors and then got on her radio. She called her unit first. She talked to her sergeant and brought him up to speed about the case of student Kristen Chambers. She told him that she had a recorded statement from a male student and that he agreed to testify on behalf of the state. In that same conversation, she told him that she would need some manpower, so to dispatch a SWAT team and a forensics team so they could be there when he comes. Finally, she told him to bring a search warrant, and he agreed.

Women's Lives Matter Too

The SWAT team came out in a full metal jacket, guns and shields when they rolled up on the scene. As soon as a uniformed officer walked on the scene, Penny escorted Conner to a cop car and placed him in the back seat.

With a search warrant in hand, Penny and a couple more cops marched toward the frat house. I wasn't able to make the trip inside, but I stood close by so I could see Tyler when they brought his ass out of the house. And five minutes later, they did just that. As a matter of fact, everyone in that house was handcuffed and brought out.

I could hear obscenities coming from Tyler's mouth the minute he was escorted out of the frat house.

"Do you know who you're fucking with? Do you know who my father is? I will have all of your jobs come tomorrow morning," he threatened.

"You're gonna need more than your father to get you out of this one," I shouted. And he heard me.

His head turned around like the girl from *The Exorcist*. "Oh, so this is about you, huh? Bitch, I didn't rape you, and when I'm done with your ass, you're gonna disappear forever." His threats continued.

"Oh, like you did Kristen Chambers and Jessica, huh? You didn't have to kill them, you fucking murderer!" I shouted. I was tearing up. How dare he say that he's gonna make me disappear too. This guy was pure evil.

Shocked by the fact that I called out those names, he went silent. Had I hit a nerve? Did he know that the cops and I are on to him?

"Don't shut up now, big mouth! Talk all your shit now! I may not be able to send your ass to jail for raping me, but I'm gonna make sure you pay for what you did to them. And once they put your ass in prison for the rest of your life, you're gonna be somebody's bitch!" I continued to shout at him. "Oh, and you're going to jail too, Eric! You fucking pussy! You did everything that bastard told you to do, and now look at you!" I yelled as Eric was escorted out of the frat house.

One by one, all the frat guys were marching in a single line, and it brought joy to me. Finally, Tyler got burned *playing with fire*. Too bad it was done at Jessica's, Gia's, and Kristen's expense, but they will never be forgotten. I can promise you that.

Epilogue

My mom called me after hearing about what happened on campus. She apologized to me for treating me the way that she's been treating me over the years. She told me how proud she was of me. She even told me that she's been jealous of me all her life because I was beautiful and confident, two things that she wasn't. She poured her heart out to me, and it felt really good to hear her say the things she was saying. I cried damn near the entire phone call. And because of everything going on, she asked me to take off the rest of the semester to come back home, and I agreed to do so.

Everyone around campus couldn't believe it when they found out that Penny Nelson was an undercover detective put there to find out where Kristen Chambers was. The two girls who shared a room with her were shocked the most. They said that Penny acted like a normal student and that they never suspected her of being anyone else.

Maria was sad to find out what really happened to Jessica and Kristen Chambers. She expressed how proud she was of me for standing up to the frat guys and helping to break the case. The news media was all over the case dealing with Tyler. He wasn't the privileged, popular guy to the university anymore. They went into PR mode and distanced themselves from the bad publicity.

When the trial was over, Tyler got two life sentences. Conner received a thirty-year prison sentence, and that was after he testified for the prosecutor. From what I heard, he's under suicide watch for threatening to kill himself. This came after he was attacked by a gang of inmates in his cell block. Eric received one hundred years with no chance of parole. There was another frat guy named Mitch Thomas. He didn't have a hand in the murders of both women, but he was convicted of being an accessory after the fact because he helped Conner and Eric put Jessica in the back of her car, so he was given five years. Plus, he was expelled from school.

The sad part about this is that those women's lives were cut short. After knowing what I know now, I can't begin to trust another man. Men will lead you down a road of chaos if you let them, and all these girls wanted was to be loved. Gia wanted to be loved. Jessica wanted to be loved. And I'm sure Kristen did too. So how can I move beyond this point? Only God knows!

More adventures to come as Yoshi Lomax
starts to make a name for herself
in
PLAYING THEIR GAMES
Coming soon
From Kiki Swinson
and
Dafina Books